Ross MacKenzie

# SHADOWSMITH

To Lydia
Happy reading!

*For Mum and Dad*

*Thank you forever*

Kelpies is an imprint of Floris Books
First published in 2016 by Floris Books
Third printing 2017
First published in the USA in 2017



The publisher acknowledges subsidy from
Creative Scotland towards the publication
of this volume

Also available as an eBook

British Library CIP data available
ISBN 978-178250-304-0
Printed & bound by MBM Print SCS Ltd, Glasgow

# ONE

# The Storm and the Spiders

# Opening the Door

There were two men in the graveyard, under the stars.

Both were very tall and unnaturally thin, and wore black suits and long black coats. They walked through the oldest parts of the church grounds among overgrown weeds and tombstones so decayed that the names of those buried beneath had been lost forever.

"This way," said the first man, who was bald and had a large crooked nose. He led the way through a tangle of trees to a wild patch of ground covered by long grass. "Here."

The second man had a face full of sharp features and a head of straggly dark hair. "You're sure?"

"Positive," said the bald-headed man. "Unconsecrated ground. There's witches here. I can smell 'em. Have you ever known my nose to be wrong?"

The dark-haired man looked around, and smiled. "I do like a good graveyard," he said. "Don't you just *love* a good graveyard, Brother Swan?"

Brother Swan, the bald man, rubbed his hands together. "I do indeed, Brother Swift. Reminds me of the old days."

"Quite so," said Brother Swift. "I mean, I remember a time when we had the power to turn countries and kings against one another just by whispering in their ears. How I long for the days when we sent plagues crawling around the world just by blowing into the wind."

"All that lovely red blood," said Brother Swan. "All that delicious pain and suffering." He licked his lips. "But look at us now, brother – reduced to sneaking about in the shadows. Mother would be turning in her grave. If she had one."

"We won't be sneaking much longer." Brother Swift shook his greasy head. "No. Soon we'll stand proud, and we'll unleash hell."

"Lovely." Brother Swan stepped forward, reached into his long black coat and pulled out three black candles. He crouched down and twisted each waxy stem into the ground. Next he struck a match and lit them, casting a soft yellow light on the surrounding trees.

Then, together, the brothers began to speak.

If you had been there, in the darkness of the graveyard, you would not have understood what they were saying. The words they spoke were a strange collection of sounds, some soft and hissing, others sharp and cutting. All of the words were ancient.

As Brothers Swan and Swift spoke, the air around them became heavy and crackled with static. The yellow flames flickered and danced and turned blue, then green, then red, bright as a flare. And then the red flames changed to black. If you could burn a shadow, this would be the colour of its flames.

They waited.

They did not move, did not speak.

The candles went out.

In front of Brother Swan and Brother Swift a long, thin crack appeared. Not a crack in the earth, in the mud and the stone. No. A crack in the *world.* A crack in *everything.* And on the other side was a faraway darkness so deep it made the night in the graveyard grow heavier. Thousands of creatures scuttled out of the crack in the world, tiny and inky-black, as if someone had lifted a stone and disturbed them.

And then the witches came.

Three shadows dragged themselves up and out of the fissure, and stood in the moonlight in front of the two brothers.

Brother Swift twisted a lock of greasy hair around a skinny finger. "You'll do," he said. "You'll do nicely."

Brother Swan looked the shadows up and down. Their shapes shifted and warped in the dim light of the moon. "Be still, my dears," he said. "Be easy. We've brought you back. Back to the world that didn't want you, the world that tormented and killed you."

One of the witches tried to speak, but her voice was nothing more than the sound of the night breeze in the long grass.

"Be calm," said Brother Swift. "Your strength will come back. And when it does it will be your turn. Your turn to get revenge, to make them suffer."

"We have a job for you," Brother Swan told the shadows. He smiled. "Now listen carefully, my dears, while I tell you all about the Shadowsmith..."

# The Girl at the Window

Kirby lay on his bed and stared at the spider on the ceiling.

*It's watching me,* he thought as the spider twitched its legs. *It's actually watching me.*

The spider was about the size of a fifty pence piece. It was blacker than black, the colour of a nightmare.

And it had been following him.

He knew it sounded mad. But for the last week it seemed like the spider was everywhere he went. Even when he couldn't see it, he could sense it. And when he thought about the spider, inside his head felt like the air just before a rainstorm, heavy and dull and full.

He was beginning to wonder if it was really there at all. Maybe it was a trick of the mind, his brain's way of distracting him from real life, from the awful thing that was happening to his family.

Two weeks had passed since the storm.

When you lived by the sea you got used to storms. They were a part of life, as normal as shopping or homework or the threat of gull droppings on your ice cream. But this one had been different. Nobody had predicted that such a violent storm would strike at the start of summer. Kirby could still hear the roar of the wind through the winding streets of Craghaven, still see the rain smashing against his classroom window. He could hear his footsteps echo in the empty school corridors and see the frightened look in his dad's eyes as he waited for Kirby in the office.

Two weeks.

The summer holidays had begun since then. His classmates were out playing in the streets or heading off on holiday with their families, full of nervous excitement at the thought of starting high school at the end of the summer. Repair work had begun on the storm-damaged buildings. The world was still turning. Life was going on.

But not for Kirby or his dad.

For them, the world would not turn again until the moment Mum woke up.

The dread of never seeing her smile again, never hearing her voice or feeling one of her hugs had consumed Kirby, filled him up until there was room for nothing else.

Until the spider had arrived.

*Clack!*

Kirby's gaze left the spider, flicked to the window.

*Clack!*

He sat up just as another stone – *clack!* – bounced off the window pane.

There was a girl in a yellow plastic raincoat down on the pavement. When she spotted him peering out at her, she smiled and waved, and motioned for him to open the window.

Kirby slid the rickety bottom half of the window upward, letting the fresh sea air into his room. The summer nights were stretching, but it was late enough that the vast sky was turning a dark, rich blue, and the reflection of the moon was molten silver on the waves.

Kirby poked his head out into the night. "Who're you?" he said. Then, trying to sound stern like his dad, he added, "What you playing at?"

"I'm Amelia," said the girl in the raincoat. "Amelia Pigeon. And I'm not playing. I'm not playing at all." Amelia Pigeon half closed her eyes. "Are you brave?"

Kirby frowned. *Am I brave?* What a weird question.

Funny though – he'd been asking himself the same thing a lot lately.

"Dunno," he said. "Hope so."

Amelia Pigeon smiled up at him, all front teeth and freckles. She looked about twelve, the same age as Kirby. "That's a good answer. Usually I find it's the ones who strut around with their chests puffed out that aren't brave at all. Not when it matters." She tilted her head to one side. "You've seen the spiders, haven't you?"

Kirby's breath caught in his throat. "There's more than one?"

"Course there's more," said Amelia. "When did you see one last?"

"A minute ago. It's gone."

Amelia shook her head. "Not gone. Never gone. Just watching."

"Watching what?"

Amelia scratched her nose. "You. They want *you* gone."

"You do know that's mental?" said Kirby.

"Think that if you want," said Amelia with a shrug. "Won't make the slightest bit of difference. Can anyone else in your house see them?"

"Don't think so. Dad hates spiders. If he'd seen one I'd have heard him swearing at it or trying to kill it with one of his shoes. When you say they want me gone..."

"Dead," said Amelia matter-of-factly. "They want you dead. I said gone because it sounds less scary."

Kirby was not usually the type of boy to be left stuck for words. But now he thought for a moment and opened his mouth, and all he could say was, "*What*?"

Amelia Pigeon reached into her yellow raincoat, and when she pulled out her hand she was holding a rough, barky twig about the length of a ruler. "Take this," she said, and she tossed it up to the window. Kirby missed it. Amelia Pigeon gave him a sharp look and tossed it again. This time he caught it.

"What is it?"

"Hazel. Picked at midnight. Simple, but it works."

Kirby examined the stick. It looked like every other stick he'd ever seen.

"They'll come soon," said Amelia. "Don't know exactly when. But they'll come. And there'll be lots of 'em."

"Lots of spiders?"

"When they come, use the hazel," Amelia went on. "Like this..." She pulled another twig from the depths of her raincoat, touched the tip to the ground, and drew an imaginary circle around herself. "They won't come inside the circle. Whatever you do, don't step outside it. And don't panic."

"But—"

"I have to go. Things I need to do. I'll be back."

"If you say so," said Kirby. He glanced at the hazel twig in his hand, and when he looked back the girl was gone.

# Visiting Time

Next morning, Kirby and his dad made the drive to the hospital a few towns away.

They sat in silence for most of the journey. Every now and then Dad would say something like, "I hear this heatwave's going to last all summer." Or, "Sea's calm today." Or even, "I hear something killed another one of Farmer Weir's sheep. Bit of a mystery, that. People are saying it's some sort of animal escaped from a zoo."

It would be fair to say that conversation between Kirby and his dad was awkward at best. When he'd been very little, Kirby remembered how they used to laugh together, how Dad would toss him in the air and catch him in his big arms. But as he'd grown, so too had the distance between them.

Kirby wasn't big or tough like his dad, who was a lobsterman and a lifeboat volunteer and probably had seawater running through his veins. Kirby was small and scrawny, and he was terrified of the vast, powerful ocean. He loved to read, to set off on magical adventures through the pages of his favourite books. The only thing Dad ever read was the sports section of the paper. He wasn't a bad dad. He wasn't cruel or unkind, not at all. But to Kirby, he was just a big, tough, lobster-fishing, sea-loving, scratchy-jumper-wearing, bearded mystery.

Kirby and Mum, on the other hand, were the very best of friends. They read together, and watched movies, and turned up the radio when a song they liked came on and sang as loud as they could.

Or at least they used to...

The smell of the hospital bothered Kirby. It was one of those smells that stuck to you long after you left, clean and cold.

Mum was too ill to be on a ward; she was in a private room on the third floor. When they arrived, Kirby and his dad were ushered in by a nurse. This was always the moment he dreaded most, that split-second of shock when he saw her lying in a strange bed connected to all those machines.

He went to the side of her bed, took her hand, squeezed it gently. "Hi Mum. It's me. Kirby."

The sting of tears made him turn away. He didn't want Dad to see him cry.

A woman in a white coat appeared at the door, a blue folder in her hands. "Mr Simpson. Do you have a few minutes?"

"Course," said Dad with a polite smile. "Will you keep Mum company for a wee bit, pal?"

When Dad stepped outside, Kirby brought a chair over and opened the drawer beside the bed, bringing out a battered old copy of *The Jungle Book*.

"Do you remember where we left off?" he said. "Course you do. Here we go then..."

He read aloud, hoping that somewhere deep down Mum could hear him, and the thought that part of her was listening made him want to keep reading. But after five minutes something stopped him, a heavy, crawling feeling in the back of his mind. He shivered, and looked around the room. The faded blue curtains by his shoulder drew his gaze.

Reaching out slowly, he pulled one curtain back.

A black spider stared at him from the wall.

Amelia Pigeon's words were still fresh: "They want you dead."

Suddenly Kirby didn't feel like reading any more. He placed the book back in the drawer, and when he peeked behind the curtain again the spider was gone.

The tide was out. Beyond Craghaven harbour, Brothers Swan and Swift stood on the dark rocks.

"What you doing?" asked Brother Swan.

Brother Swift had sat down and was removing his shoes and socks. "I'm having a paddle. Care to join me?" He stood up and walked a little further down the rocks, to the place where the sea broke on the land in gentle, lapping waves. When he dipped his foot in the water, it steamed and bubbled.

"I prefer to keep my tootsies dry, thank you very much," said Brother Swan. He ran his fingers over his bald head, picked a scab off his scalp with filthy fingernails and examined it. Then he popped it into his mouth. He walked to the edge of the rocks, being careful not to get his feet wet, and pointed out to sea, to a wedge-shaped, rocky island a kilometre or so off the coast. "You're sure that's the place?"

Brother Swift stood shin-deep in the North Sea, the legs of his black trousers rolled up to reveal skinny legs the colour of rotten milk. "I'm sure," he said. "That's it alright. That's where we make our final move."

"Everything's set," said Brother Swan. "The witches are ready. Now it's up to her."

"She'll find them," said Brother Swift. "Don't worry about that. And when she does, all we have to do is sit back and watch the fireworks."

# The Swarm

Kirby woke at three minutes past midnight. He was still in that strange place between asleep and awake where everything and nothing make sense all at once, when he felt a slow creeping sensation on his face.

His heart gave a jolt. He pawed something off his skin and fell out of bed, landing on the floor with a thump.

The air had turned icy cold. Kirby's breath danced in silver curls around his head in the pale moonlight, which stole in through a crack in the curtains.

Even in the gloom he could see the spiders on the ceiling. They were darker than the night, and each time he blinked he saw more of them.

The spider that had been on his face was still on his bed. It was the biggest he'd ever seen, with thick hairy legs and a fat body. It had beady green eyes and it locked Kirby in its gaze.

Kirby stifled a scream. Every fibre, every muscle was urging him to run. But he knew somehow if he did, that would be the end of it. The end of him.

Slowly, silently, he reached for the hazel twig on his bedside drawer and held it out towards the spider on the bed, his hands shaking, his heart about to burst through his chest.

The spider backed away.

"*Yessss!*" Kirby whispered and jumped up and down in a mini victory dance.

But the battle had only just begun.

By now there were twenty or thirty spiders on the ceiling. Kirby shivered at the sight of them. They made his skin crawl, his teeth prickle, his gums itch. He shifted from foot to foot, waving the wand frantically towards them. "Take that!"

All the spiders flinched and crept back.

Kirby punched the air. Perhaps he *could* do this.

He touched the hazel twig to the carpet, and drew an imaginary circle around himself just as Amelia Pigeon had shown him. There he stood, hardly daring to breathe, watching the first spiders lower themselves to the floor and approach him.

They came closer and closer, and just when it seemed they were going to swarm him, they stopped, each and every one of them, as if an invisible wall was preventing them from moving any further. The spiders gathered in a ring around him, prodding at the air with their legs, twitching angrily.

Despite the icy fear in his chest, Kirby looked at the hazel twig in his hands and laughed. He kissed it, grasping it so tightly his knuckles turned the colour of bone.

*Thank you Amelia Pigeon!*

All at once there was an angry rushing sound, a blast of cold air, and spiders began to pour in from the window, hundreds of them: a waterfall of inky creatures flooding his room.

Kirby yelped and jumped inside his little circle. He could do nothing but watch, his hand over his mouth, his eyes wide, as the tide of spiders rose. They crawled over everything – his bookcase, his bed, his computer desk – and they clambered on top of each other, layer upon layer, until his entire room was coated in a seething black mass.

All but a little island of carpet, on which Kirby Simpson stood stranded, alone in a sea of nightmares.

# Alone in the Dark

Kirby's first thought was to yell for his dad, but he quickly got over that. He would not put anyone else in danger.

His second thought was Amelia Pigeon. She knew about the spiders, knew how to deal with them. Maybe somehow she'd know he was in trouble. Maybe she was on her way to help.

"They won't come inside the circle," she'd told him. "Whatever you do, don't step outside it."

Kirby nodded to himself. "Stay inside the circle," he repeated over and over.

It was more difficult than it sounded. The ring of spiders was tightly wrapped around him. He wished he'd drawn a bigger circle, one in which he could at least sit comfortably. As it was, there was barely enough space to sit cross-legged.

The second problem – quite a biggie when you

thought about it – was that Amelia Pigeon hadn't told him what to do *after* he was inside the circle. Was it a case of waiting the spiders out? Hoping they'd lose interest? He stole a glance up at them; they stared intently back, green eyes blazing. Somehow he didn't see that happening.

Should he ask them what they wanted? Try and negotiate? That's what the police would do in the movies he'd seen. But *they* weren't dealing with a horde of nightmare spiders, were they?

As a multitude of thoughts passed through his mind the spiders watched and waited, and Kirby clung desperately to his knees to stop himself toppling out of the circle. He lost all sense of time in the dark. Each tick of the clock was a forever.

And then, as the night grew darkest, the dry scratch of the spiders' legs became a whisper, and a voice as arid as a desert spoke to him.

"She's leaving you," it said.

At first Kirby did not understand. But the voice went on, "Your mother – she wants to leave."

"Shut up," said Kirby.

"If she wanted to stay with you, why is she lying in a bed letting it beat her?"

Kirby's throat clogged with anger, his eyes began to burn. "She's fighting as much as she can."

"Not enough," said the voice of the spiders. "You're angry at her, aren't you? Angry that she's going away..."

"I'm not!" said Kirby. But anger *was* bubbling in him. The spiders were right: part of him, the selfish part, had been upset with Mum. Why couldn't she just wake up? What was stopping her? Didn't she want to come back to him?

"Your dad doesn't know you. He'll never understand a silly boy who's scared of the sea. You'll be a big weight round his neck... you'll drown him..."

"Go away!" yelled Kirby. "I know what you're doing. You're trying to make me leave the circle. I won't!"

"We're telling the truth," said the voice of the spiders. "You know we're right."

The words were like broken glass, stabbing at Kirby, making him wince. He wiped the tears from his eyes, and as he did he noticed the first rays of dawn squeezing through the gap in his curtains, splashing on the floor.

A wave of anger crept through the sea of spiders.

Kirby looked from the spiders to the sunlight and back. "You don't like the sun, do you?"

Daylight was creeping further into the room.

Kirby heard his dad, who was always up with the sun, moving around in the bathroom.

"This is not finished," said the spiders. "You are ours, Kirby Simpson. It's just a matter of time."

Kirby blinked, and the spiders vanished.

He dropped to his knees and closed his eyes. "Thank you." He lay on his belly and kissed the small patch of carpet that had been his island. "Thank you. Thank you, thank you, thank you, thank—"

The bedroom door creaked open.

Kirby looked up, his lips still puckered.

Dad stood in the doorway wearing an expression that said, *I wish I understood my son.*

"Toast'll be waiting, pal," he said, and he turned with a shrug and walked away.

# An Invitation to Certain Death... Maybe

The toast was indeed waiting, piled high on a plate on the kitchen table. Kirby searched through the blackened slices for a piece that was less burnt than the others. The quality of toast in the household had gone downhill since Mum's accident. He spread some raspberry jam on what was basically a piece of charcoal, took one bite, and quickly washed it down with a glug of orange juice.

"Have you phoned the hospital yet?" he asked.

Dad looked up from his toast. There were dark circles around his eyes, and Kirby thought he looked much older than he had a few weeks ago.

"Aye. No change. I suppose no news is good news though, eh?"

They sat in silence for a while.

"So," Dad pushed his toast around his plate, "are you... you know..." He shook his head, struggling to find the words he wanted. "How are you, Kirby?"

In his head, Kirby said, *How am I? How do you think I am, Dad? Mum is in a coma and we don't know if she'll ever wake up. I probably have more in common with the lobsters you catch than I do with you. Oh! And by the way, I've just spent the entire night trying not to be killed by some sort of talking, mutant, man-eating spiders!*

Out loud he said, "I'm fine. Really, Dad. Don't worry."

Dad stood up and squeezed Kirby's shoulders with hands that felt like stone. He shrugged his bodywarmer on.

"Where are you going?"

"I'll only be ten minutes. Putting an ad up in the post office. We need someone running the boat until... until Mum wakes up. Lobsters aren't going to catch themselves, are they?" His face crumpled, and in that moment Kirby could see his dad was struggling to hold everything together, to run the house, and his lobster boat, and be there for Mum, and for Kirby.

Maybe the spiders were right. Maybe it was too much. What if he didn't want to look after Kirby by himself? What if Kirby was nothing but a big weight around his neck, choking him? Kirby wanted to run over and hug him, to explain all of his fears and hear his dad say everything would be OK.

But he didn't. He just let him go, and watched from the kitchen window until Dad disappeared round the bend, up the steep winding road towards the main street. Then Kirby turned to look the other way, down the hill to the harbour, and saw an unmistakable yellow raincoat coming round the corner. Amelia Pigeon waved at him cheerfully as she walked up the hill.

Kirby rushed to the front door to meet her.

"Oh good," she said. "You're still alive."

"Yeah. Hello. There are some questions I really want to ask you."

Amelia's eyes widened. "The spiders came, didn't they?"

"How did you know what would happen?"

"Somebody has to know." She looked quite pleased with herself. "Guess what else? I found the nest!"

Thinking about a nest full of those things made Kirby itch.

"We should tell someone. The police... or the army. They could torch 'em with flame-throwers! Blow them up with missiles..." Kirby stopped when he saw the pitying look on Amelia Pigeon's face.

And then it dawned on him. It was obvious, really, when he thought about it.

"Nobody else can see the spiders, can they?" he asked. "Just you and me. That's why they want me gone."

Amelia's eyes lit up, large and green. "You're beginning to catch on."

"So why can I see them? I'm mental, aren't I? I knew it..."

"You're not mental," said Amelia. "Just tuned in to the right channel. Or the wrong one, depending on how you see it." She half closed her eyes again, like she'd done the night they met, and looked him up and down as if she was measuring him. "I'm going to get rid of the nest. You want to come?"

"How are you going to get rid of it?" said Kirby.

"Let me worry about that bit. But I might need you to bring me back. Sometimes it takes a lot out of me." Amelia looked very serious, and her eyes seemed to grow older, deeper. "The spiders," she said, "are just the start. There's worse to come. Things you couldn't imagine, not even in your worst nightmares."

Kirby stared at this strange girl in her yellow raincoat. "Who *are* you?"

Amelia smiled. "You know all those stories about phantoms and bogeymen and things that go bump in the night? They're true, Kirby. They're real.

But even monsters have to be scared of something. And that something is me."

Kirby felt a strange sort of charge in the air as she spoke.

"Well, whoever you are, I don't know how you think I'll be able to help," he said. "I'm nothing special. I'm just me."

"Ha!" said Amelia. "'Just me' indeed! I know all about you, Kirby Simpson." She poked his chest with a finger. "I see what you've got in there. And I know you're hurting. I know you're having a hard time of it. Maybe an adventure isn't the worst thing that could happen right now, mmm?"

It was a glorious day. The sun was climbing through the endless sky, shattering in fragments upon the waves. The clean air filled Kirby's lungs, tasted of salt and, this morning, of something else, something far away and exotic, something that made his heart beat faster, made him stand taller.

Adventure.

"I'll get dressed," he said.

# Into the Dark

Twenty minutes later they were walking past the harbour, pinching their noses at the stink of lobster creels cooking in the summer heat.

"Where's the nest?" asked Kirby.

"Not far," said Amelia in a bright voice. She was marching just ahead of him. Kirby stared at the back of her head.

"Just now, at my house, you said you know I'm having a hard time. *How* do you know?"

She shrugged. "Just do. I know stuff. For example: Mrs Coppershot, the old lady who stays on Harbour Street next door to you? Talks to her garden gnomes."

Kirby scoffed. "She does not!"

"And she has names for them all. The one with the orange hat is Mr Wibbles. The little one with the fishing rod is Fishy McSqueak."

"Are you serious?" said Kirby through a laugh.

"Cross my heart."

Kirby's smile vanished. "So you know about Mum then?"

Amelia slowed so that they were side by side. She fixed him with bright green eyes and nodded. "I know she was hurt during the storm."

"She works in the library," said Kirby. "It's a really old building. The roof fell in on top of her. Can you help her?" The question spilled from his lips before he could give it any thought, and he felt foolish.

Amelia smiled at him, but the smile was sad around the edges. "There's some journeys must be walked alone, Kirby." She was quiet for a moment. "But she's not gone. Not yet. You remember that."

On they walked, through the hole in the harbour wall, down the rough rock steps to Ruby Cove, a crescent of steep red cliffs towering over a thin strip of sand. They followed the beach as far as they could, to where the foot of the cliffs stretched out towards the sea in a vein of craggy red rocks. Everything smelled of sunshine and sand. Amelia climbed over the rocks and dropped out of sight.

On the other side of the rocks the sea was lapping against a small rowing boat covered in peeling red paint and hardened gull droppings. Amelia was already inside, sitting with an oar in each hand.

Kirby stared at the boat. His stomach shrunk to

about the size of a grape. “I don’t like the sea.”

Amelia looked all around. “Ha! You picked the perfect place to grow up then, eh? Can you swim?”

“Yeah,” said Kirby. “I mean. I’m OK down the leisure centre. But the sea… it’s big and deep and you never know what’s swimming under you.”

“Well you won’t have to go in the actual water.” Amelia frowned. “Unless they chew a hole through the boat. Hadn’t thought of that.”

Kirby hoped she was joking, but suspected not.

“I’m leaving in ten seconds,” she said, “whether you’re on this boat or not.” She reached down into the boat and tossed him a life jacket.

“How far is it?”

“Seven seconds… six…”

Kirby scrambled into the life jacket, wondering why he was even thinking about going along. His fear of deep water was one of the things that sometimes made him think there’d been a mix-up at the hospital, and that he secretly belonged to another family.

“Three…

two…

one…”

Kirby leapt off the rocks, landing with a thud in the boat, which bobbed and rocked under him.

“Good,” said Amelia with a bright smile. She untied

the boat from a crag in the rock and off they set.

She was a surprisingly strong rower, cutting through the water with ease. "Nice and calm today."

"Is it?" Kirby was fighting the urge to vomit over the side.

They'd been out for maybe twenty minutes when Amelia looked over her shoulder and nodded. "There."

It was a sea cave. The entrance was narrow, but Amelia had no trouble guiding the boat in. She stopped just inside the mouth. "You OK?"

Kirby stared past her, into the blackness. Memories of the spiders scuttled across his mind. He began to shiver. Amelia let the oars rest on the boat and took his hands.

"You listen here. Being brave isn't about not feeling afraid. Being brave is admitting you're frightened, and standing up to it."

The touch of her hands was warm. Kirby sat up a little straighter. "What do we need to do?"

"Just get me out of here once it's done. Don't panic, don't try to wake me if I pass out. Got it?"

Kirby nodded.

Then Amelia Pigeon picked up the oars and began to row, and they were swallowed by the waiting dark.

# Pest Control

"Here," said Amelia, handing Kirby a torch. He flicked it on, and a reassuring beam of clean light cut through the cave.

The winding path of the cavern led them deeper.

"How far back does it go?"

Amelia did not answer. A change had come over her; her eyes had taken on a deep, serious quality again, a fierce look of wisdom and confidence. The air around the boat seemed to crackle.

As Kirby shone the flashlight around, things scurried on the cave walls.

Around another few bends, Amelia slowed, letting the boat drift and bringing the oars up. "Switch the torch off," she said.

"We'll be blind."

"Switch it off, boy."

Kirby gripped the torch tight. A familiar sound

filled his ears, dry and creeping, like dead leaves in the breeze, and the stench of rot was thick in the air. He flicked the torch off, and to his surprise he could still see. Amelia had steered them to an underground chamber, bathed in a faint green glow.

The nest was hanging above them.

It was huge and spherical, constructed from strands of webbing that gave off a sickly greenish light. Something inside the nest moved, something very big and very heavy, causing the nest to quiver and swing.

"What's inside?" he asked.

"Hopefully we won't find out. Now be quiet and let me think."

All around the nest, criss-crossing in uncountable tangles and knots, were glowing webs, each belonging to a spider. There were thousands of them. Tens of thousands. They flickered and seemed to change shape constantly, flitting between spider form and something else, something squirming and hungry.

There were things caught in the webs. Things from the world Kirby knew: bats and birds wrapped in glowing silk, half eaten.

The dark was shattered by a short burst of sound, a screeching scream coming from inside the nest. It made Kirby cover his ears, made his legs buckle.

Silence.

He stared up at the nest and almost fell back when he caught sight of something shifting inside, something huge and many-legged. Its shining eyes, hundreds of them, sparkled in the glow of the nest. Whatever the spiders were, and they were not spiders, not really, this thing in the nest was the worst of them.

"What now?"

Amelia reached into her yellow raincoat and pulled out her hazel twig. She leaned over the edge of the rowing boat, dipped the tip of the twig into the water, and dragged it all the way round the boat.

As soon as she was done the creatures came.

They dropped from their webs, all glowing and flickering. They hung around the boat in a pulsing curtain of silk.

Kirby screamed, and the twitching curtain closed in. His heartbeat was pounding in his ears, his body numb with fear and cold. He tried to breathe, found himself choking, gasping for clean air.

Amelia grabbed him by the shoulders. "Don't let them into your head!"

Kirby looked into her eyes, and felt a spark of relief warm his chest. She wasn't frightened – she could handle this.

"You'll be fine," she said. "Just don't do anything stupid, like fall in the water."

Amelia smiled, let go of him and spun round the boat, her hazel wand aloft. The curtain of creatures collapsed into the water in a fizzing shower of sparks. Then she pointed the hazel towards the nest and began to speak.

Kirby strained to listen, caught small snippets of what she was saying, but he did not understand. These were old words – somehow he knew that – words from the beginning of the world. And as Amelia spoke them – or was she singing? – Kirby remembered things long forgotten, saw secrets buried by time. But it was too much to hold in his head, too painful to know, and it slipped away...

As Amelia continued to speak, the remaining spiders grew frantic. There was a creak from the roof of the cave as the nest began to swing. Strands of silk were fraying and snapping like rotten rope, spiders dropping into the water.

The thing inside the nest screeched back, it's eyes now glowing red with hatred.

"Who let you in?" Amelia shouted out. "Who opened the door to this world?"

The creature's grating voice echoed around the cave. "We came when they let the others in," it said.

"We took our chance when the gap opened. We left the forever nothingness and found this world."

"Others?" said Amelia. "What others?"

"Witches," said the voice.

The centre of the nest dropped with a jerk and swung wildly, hanging on by the thinnest of threads, then broke away from the rock ceiling. As it smashed through the surface of the water Kirby glimpsed one of the enormous hairy legs of the creature within, and gulped.

The boat banged against the cave wall, throwing Kirby to the floor. He heard something then that scared him even more than the creature in the nest. He heard Amelia Pigeon, and there was fear in her voice.

"No!" she was yelling. "No, no, no, no, NO!" She was leaning over the boat, reaching for something in the water. Kirby pulled himself up, strained to see what she was trying to get.

It was the hazel twig. Their protection. A knife of panic stuck him in the gut.

"Don't you have another?"

"I gave it to you yesterday! Didn't you bring it?"

"Erm... no."

Without the hazel keeping them at bay, the spiders began to rain down on the rowing boat, with a pitter-patter as they landed on the wood. They fell on Kirby, in his hair, on his face, in his clothes, and as they crawled all over him, he heard a terrified wail. It took him a moment to realise the sound was coming from him.

The spiders were spinning silk around him, binding him in their web. He tried to shake the fear from his body. Remembering the torch in his pocket, he switched it on, shining the light on his own face, sending the spiders scurrying.

On the other side of the boat Amelia was still trying to retrieve the hazel, but she stretched too far and went toppling into the water.

Kirby reacted without thinking. He shrugged off the growing webs and clambered forward, reaching out over the water. "Grab my hand, Amelia!"

She swam up and grasped it, and he dragged her aboard, coughing and choking. Then he turned back and reached for the twig. His fingertips touched it, and he strained against the boat, stretching further and further still, until at last his hand closed around it.

One of the spiders landed on his hand then, and seemed to bite him. There was a flash of burning pain like nothing he'd ever experienced. He screamed out, but he did not let go of the stick. He dragged the tip of it through the water, and when the circle around the boat was complete, the spiders inside stopped, exploding in tiny flashes of flame, leaving behind nothing but scorch marks and ash.

Amelia had recovered. She was back on her feet, soaked through, silhouetted against the glow from the nest. "Thank you Kirby," she said gravely as she took the hazel, pointed it at the nest, and spoke her words again.

The nest bobbed and shivered in the water, glowed brighter and brighter, so dazzling it hurt Kirby's eyes. The creature inside shrieked and spat and the water around the nest sizzled and churned, until the thing was finally defeated and was swallowed by black water.

Kirby watched over the edge of the boat as it sank to the bottom, its glow becoming fainter, until the cave was dark once more.

Everything was still. The spiders were gone. Kirby could hear nothing but his own gasping breath. He picked up the torch, fumbled with it and switched it on, turning the light towards Amelia.

Her wet hair was plastered to her head. She rubbed her hands together, a look of satisfaction on her freckled face. "Well now. That about takes care of that."

And then she collapsed.

# What Happened Next

Kirby did as Amelia asked. He got her out of the cave.

It wasn't easy; he'd never rowed a boat in his life. A lot of the time the oars thrashed ineffectively in the water, or took him in the wrong direction or in circles. But he got there.

When the boat floated out of the darkness into the warm morning sunshine, his chest swelled with relief and happiness.

Amelia began to stir in the daylight. Kirby scrambled over and helped her onto the seat.

"You OK?"

Amelia nodded. "Ice cream," she said. "I want ice cream."

Kirby rowed as fast as he could. His arms and chest burned, and even though the sea was calm it took him three times as long as Amelia to row the distance back to land. By the time they reached the red rocks at Ruby Cove, Amelia was sitting up, staring out at the water.

Kirby hopped out of the boat, looped the rope over a piece of jutting rock, and helped Amelia ashore.

"Can you walk?"

She nodded. Kirby took her hand and led her slowly along the beach, back up the hill to the harbour and into Frankie's Café.

They shared a caramel-chocolate-brownie ice-cream sundae – cold ice cream, warm caramel and chunks of chocolate brownie swirling around in their mouths.

"Better?" asked Kirby.

Amelia managed a smile. Some of the colour had returned to her face.

Warbling waltz music filled the café, accompanied by the sound of Frankie, the owner, singing as he cooked bacon and eggs on the grill for the workmen who were repairing the harbour wall.

Amelia leaned her elbows on the table. "I'm sorry."

"Sorry?"

"I promised you'd be safe."

Kirby chewed on another chunk of brownie. "I *am* safe."

"No thanks to me. I made a mistake. I was careless.

If you hadn't been so quick, fetching the wand, I'm not sure what would've happened."

Between the adrenaline from his adventure and the vast amounts of sugar he was shovelling into his face, Kirby was in no mood to be glum. In fact, this was the happiest he'd been since the storm. It wasn't that he'd stopped worrying about Mum – the worry was always there, niggling and gnawing like toothache – but when Amelia was around it eased and faded.

"I'm *fine*," he said. "I didn't get eaten..."

"But you could've been."

"Aye, but I didn't! I'm here, eating ice cream. The monsters are gone..." He trailed off, watching her expression darken. "They *are* gone, aren't they? No more black spidery things?"

"No. None of those."

"See! Happy days!"

Amelia did not crack a smile. "Creatures like the spiders are never supposed to come here in the first place, Kirby. They're from... somewhere else. A dark place." Amelia stared off into the distance, as if she was recalling far-off memories. "You heard that thing in the nest. Someone opened the door. The question is who?"

"I'll help you find out," said Kirby cheerfully.

"No, you will not. It's far too dangerous. What you will do is go and wash the ice cream off your face. It's in your eyebrows. How is that even possible?"

Kirby stared across the table at her. "Are you a witch?"

Amelia sat back in her seat, folded her arms. "I am precisely what I am, Kirby Simpson," she said. "And that's the end of it."

"But—"

"Ice cream. Eyebrows. Now."

Kirby was going to argue, but fighting with Amelia was like fighting with an adult: always a losing battle, even if you were right. He huffed out of the booth, went to the toilet and cleaned his face. When he returned to the table, Amelia's seat was empty.

"Frankie," he said, rushing to the counter, "what happened to the girl I was with?"

Frankie flipped an egg over on the grill. He turned around and smiled. "Sweet girl. She paid the bill and left... Got yourself a girlfriend, Kirby?"

The workmen at the nearest table chuckled. Kirby felt his face redden.

"Nope!" he yelled as he ran for the door.

The late-morning sun was baking the world. Kirby shaded his eyes as he looked around, hoping to catch a glimpse of Amelia's yellow raincoat.

She was not across the street at the harbour. He ran down to Ruby Cove but couldn't find her. He searched the maze of roads and alleyways that made up Craghaven, but she was nowhere to be seen.

It seemed Amelia Pigeon had vanished.

Back in the café, nobody noticed the two tall men dressed in black who sat in a booth by the far wall. Brother Swan and Brother Swift had been watching Amelia and Kirby with great interest.

"She knows we're here," said Brother Swan, wiping his long fingers over his bald head.

"She doesn't," said Brother Swift. "She suspects, is all."

"She's getting rusty," said Brother Swan. "I remember a time when she'd have sniffed us out and sent us back to the darkness before her friend had finished his sickly sundae."

"She's not what she once was," agreed Brother Swift, "I'll grant you. But she's still strong enough for what we need."

"I hope you're right, dear brother."

They stood up, and walked to the door. On the way, Brother Swan reached over a workman's shoulder, touching the bacon on his plate with a pale finger. Nobody noticed.

"Couldn't resist," he said.

"Stomach bug?" asked Brother Swift. "Oh, you've always been an artist when it comes to disorders of the digestive system."

"It's good to be back." Brother Swan smiled as he walked through the solid door, out towards the harbour.

# TWO

# The Woods

# The Scar

Three days went by, and without Amelia Pigeon and her adventures to distract him, thoughts of Mum filled Kirby's head once again. It seemed everything in the house, every room, every object was attached to a memory. The notches on the kitchen door where she'd marked his height every birthday. The broken branch on the apple tree in their narrow garden where she'd insisted on having a go on the rope swing. The hall mirror where they'd leave each other secret messages scrawled in foggy breath.

Dad was doing his best; Kirby knew that. But no matter how they both tried, they could not escape the fact that the house was filled with Mum's absence, the smell of Dad's burnt toast and the sound of awkward silence.

"What you reading?" Dad asked one warm

Wednesday night, when the salty sea air breathed through the open windows.

Kirby, lying on his belly on the living-room floor, said, "*Coraline*."

"Any good?"

"Really good."

A pause.

"Never been much of a reader myself."

"I know."

Another pause.

"Maybe you could... I dunno... help me with that. We could read your book together. What is it... *Caroline*?"

"*Coraline*."

"Right. So what do you think?"

Yet another pause.

"You don't have to do this, Dad."

"Do what?"

"Try so hard. It's fine."

Dad sat up a little straighter. He frowned. "Well maybe I want to."

"You've never been interested before," said Kirby. Anger was bubbling up in his chest, though he knew Dad wasn't doing anything wrong.

Dad looked sad and annoyed at the same time. "That's not fair. I just want to help you."

Kirby stood up and closed his book. "I don't need help, I need Mum." And he stormed away up the stairs, slamming his door and collapsing on his bed.

He knew he hadn't been fair, knew Dad was only trying to be there for him. But Kirby was just so angry at everything, at Mum and Dad and Amelia and the world. He had to let it out or he felt he might explode.

Sometime later, maybe ten minutes, maybe an hour, Kirby heard the creak of his dad's footsteps in the hallway outside. He waited for the knock on the door. But it didn't come. Dad creaked away down the hall again, and Kirby lay on his bed and read his book until he fell asleep.

He woke in the night with a searing pain in the palm of his hand. His pyjamas were soaked with sweat. He reached over, fumbling with the bedside lamp, and held his trembling hand out in the light.

On the fleshy part of his palm, beneath the thumb, there was an angry red scar in the shape of a spider. Under the skin, something was skittering and pushing upward. Something was trying to get out.

Kirby would have screamed, would have called for

help, but he was so terrified that all he could do was clamp his free hand around his wrist and watch as his skin stretched outwards, the spider legs probing from inside.

Somewhere in the fog of terror, a memory flashed in his mind: back in the darkness of the sea cave, as he had reached into the water for Amelia's hazel wand, something had bitten him. A knife-sharp spider leg pierced his skin, and another, and a third. Kirby could feel the creature pushing harder, trying to squeeze out into the world. His blood was on fire. The room was moving around him, spinning, the walls closing in...

Kirby fell backwards, and it seemed to him that he had fallen through his bed, through the world he knew, of light and dark and warmth and cold and flesh and blood, to a place with none of that. And there was something with him in the nothingness, something huge and hungry and smiling, something older than he could imagine. He felt it. It was inside his head, in his mind and memories, everywhere at once...

And then there was a glimmer of light. As Kirby moved towards it he realised that he was no longer floating in the dark. He was standing in a field of corn under a night sky alive with blinking stars.

Ahead was a crumbling old farmhouse, a place he had seen before. The glimmer of light was, in fact, a yellow raincoat, hanging on the outside of the door...

In the morning when he woke up, back in his own bed, the first thing Kirby did was check his hand. He expected to find blood and a ragged, open wound where the spider had forced its way through his skin.

But he found nothing. Not a scratch, not even a mark.

He prodded the flesh beneath his thumb, watching for something beneath the skin to squirm.

Nothing happened.

Kirby lay back again, staring at the ceiling. He was sure it had not been a dream.

Then he remembered the field, and the old farmhouse, and he became sure of something else.

He knew where to find Amelia.

# The Farmhouse

The farmhouse had been a ruin for many years, since well before Kirby was born. The Weir family, who owned the land, had built a new house on the other side of their spread, with views of the cold North Sea, and through time the old house had been vandalised and damaged. The farm itself was just outside of town, perched on rolling land that became the cliffs and then the sea.

It didn't take long for Kirby to walk there. He cut down a dirt lane until he found the place he was looking for, a field filled with corn taller than a man, on the edge of thick, dark woodland.

The house sat at the far end of the field, bordering the woods. The yard was overgrown to the point of being a jungle, and thorns and nettles stung Kirby as he pushed through. Most of the windows were broken, and part of the old house was nothing more than a blackened shell, burnt away by a fire at some point in the past. He looked through a window and saw nothing inside but empty darkness, dust and shadow. But the front door was still whole and solid. Kirby knocked.

"Hello?" he said. "Amelia?"

No reply.

The door was not locked, but it was stiff. Kirby leaned against it, put his shoulder into it, pushed – and it suddenly gave way, sending him stumbling to the floor. He stood up and dusted himself off, then he looked around.

What he saw was not the same bare darkness that he'd glimpsed through the window. He was standing in a comfortable, warm farmhouse kitchen, golden sunlight streaming through the windows, the smell of toasting bread in the air.

Amelia Pigeon stood at the range, stirring the contents of a pot. She was wearing a flowery dress and a pair of Wellingtons, her yellow raincoat hanging on a hook by the door. She stared across the kitchen at Kirby.

"You don't give in easily, do you?"

"Saw this place in a dream," said Kirby. "Sort of guessed you'd be here."

She stirred the pot, still staring at him, almost

through him. "Well, you've got a knack for this, that's for sure. There's not many folk could have found me here. And I suppose if I was to send you away and move somewhere else you'd only track me down again?"

Kirby smiled. Then he looked at his hand, at the place the scar had been. "Back in the cave," he said, "when I was getting the wand out the water... something happened. I think one of those spider things bit me."

Amelia stopped stirring the pot. She frowned, took a deep breath. "Come here. Let me see."

Kirby gave her his hand, and she took it in hers and raised it close to her face. She examined every part of it, fingernails to palms. Then she sniffed at it, her freckled nose twitching.

"What's that?" asked Kirby. "What you doing?"

"Checking." Amelia's nose hovered over the place the scar had been, and she sniffed at it again, like a dog. Then, before he knew what was happening, she was dragging him towards the door and reaching into that yellow raincoat. She brought out a new hazel wand, pointed it at his hand and wiggled it about a bit.

"The good news," she said, "is you'll get to keep your hand – I think."

"You think?" Kirby pulled his hand away. "Think?"

"If it starts to blacken and shrivel up, you let me know."

"Shrivel up?"

"One of them hid inside you, Kirby." She pursed her lips and shook her head. "Clever thing. It's escaped now."

"Let's just go back to the part where I might need my hand cutting off, shall we?"

"Oh, I'm sure that won't happen." Amelia's eyes went back to his hand. "That's not your writing hand, is it?"

"Amelia!"

"I'm joking! Your hand is fine. But this settles it: I'm going to have to keep you close. Keep an eye on you. That spider's still out there. Chances are, without its brothers and sisters around it'll have fled. But just in case, you should have your hazel with you at all times. If it comes back, we'll take care of it together."

"OK." Kirby wriggled his fingers. They seemed fine. "So does this mean you're stuck with me? Whatever happens?"

"I suppose it does," said Amelia. "Here. Sit down and have some breakfast. You'll need your strength for what's ahead."

They sat at the kitchen table and ate scrambled

eggs and toast. It might have been the most delicious meal Kirby had ever tasted. The eggs were light and rich and buttery, the toast thick and golden, not even the slightest bit burnt.

As he ate, Amelia watched him with great curiosity. At last she said, "Aren't you going to ask about this place? How it's different inside than out?"

Kirby chewed his toast and shrugged. "You're a witch. You won't come out and say it but I think it's true." He looked around. "You know magic. That's what this place is. A spell or something."

Amelia chuckled. "And that doesn't bother you? Or amaze you?"

"You kidding?" said Kirby. "After the couple of days I've had, I'm just glad to be somewhere nothing wants to kill me."

Amelia's smile faded. "Um... that probably won't last long."

Kirby pushed the last few pieces of his breakfast around his plate. There was something on his mind that just wouldn't go away.

"Are you *sure* you can't help my mum?" he said at last.

Amelia stopped chewing. She swallowed her toast, and wiped the corners of her mouth. "I'm not a doctor."

"No," said Kirby, "you're more powerful. Can't you use your magic to wake her up?"

"People are too fragile," Amelia told him. Then, before he could protest, she said, "If I was to try, I might drive her mad, or kill her. It's easy to take people apart with magic. But it's almost impossible to rebuild them."

Kirby wondered what she meant by 'take people apart' and how she knew it was easy to do such a thing, but he did not ask. Part of him sensed something in Amelia, something bubbling under the surface – sadness, or darkness, or both. He didn't want to stir it up.

"All of this," she said, "started with the storm. That's what caught my attention."

"The storm?"

Kirby was sliding towards the edge of the seat, leaning his elbows on the table.

"Someone brought the storm here. Someone who wanted to cause damage – suffering."

"Well they did a good job."

Amelia nodded. She screwed up her face. "Something big is going on." She tapped her forehead. "But I can't see it. It's all squiggly and bemuddled." She held up three fingers. "Three witches. That's part of it."

"Witches? Like you?"

"No, Kirby. Not like me at all. And there's much more to it than that."

A jagged thought lodged in Kirby's brain. "These witches caused the storm? They're the reason Mum is hurt?"

"I think so," said Amelia.

A flush of anger spread through Kirby's body, crawled upwards from his toes. And then another idea occurred. "Is that why Mum isn't getting better? Is it because these witches are still out there? Do they have some sort of hold over her?"

Amelia mulled this over. "It might be possible. I've heard stranger things. Part of her might be tangled in the darkness. Lost."

Kirby raised his eyebrows. For the first time in weeks, green shoots of hope broke through the blackened surface of his thoughts. "So if we stop the witches Mum might get better?"

"I never said that."

"But it's possible?"

"Unlikely." She stared at him, her eyes tired. "You mustn't pin all of your hopes on this."

The farmhouse kitchen faded away in Kirby's mind, and he pictured his mum lying in her hospital bed, heard the beep of the machines keeping her alive.

"These witches," he said. "How do we find them?"

Amelia stood up, walked to the door and put on her yellow raincoat.

"Come with me."

# Counting Sheep

Kirby followed Amelia Pigeon away from the house and the woods, to the other side of the farm and a field of grazing sheep.

"What if the farmer catches us?" Farmer Weir was famous for chasing intruders from his land by bearing down on them in his tractor. The older kids would sometimes dare each other to run through the fields.

"Oh, he won't notice us." Amelia climbed over the gate, landing on dry grass. "Come on then."

Up and over the gate Kirby went, walking among the sheep.

"I never really got the point of sheep," Amelia said. "I mean, what are they for? What do they do?"

"What are *we* doing?" asked Kirby.

"Looking," said Amelia. "Just up here, I think." Then her eyes fixed on something in the distance and she pursed her lips and said, "I knew it. Another one."

"Another what?"

At first it looked like someone had left a pile of rags on the grass, but as they drew closer Kirby could see that the grass around the rags had turned red. Closer still and he realised what he was looking at. Or what it used to be. He felt sick.

"What would do that to a sheep?" He covered his mouth. Flies were buzzing around what was left of the carcass. He stared at Amelia and his eyes widened as he put two and two together. "One of your witches did that? It looks like it's been ripped apart by... by a bear or something!" Then he remembered what his dad had told him, about rumours of a wild animal in the woods. "You said 'another one'. How many sheep has this witch killed?"

Amelia crouched down and touched the bloodstained grass, rubbing it between her fingers. "Ten by my count. But I'm not sure why. Why would a witch bother with sheep?"

Kirby suddenly felt very sorry for Mr Weir. He didn't suppose the farmer could run off a witch in his tractor as easily as he could a group of mischievous teenagers.

"One of them is nearby," Amelia said. "In the woods, I think. I'm going after her tonight."

Kirby grimaced at what was left of the sheep. "Take me with you."

Amelia stared at him. Kirby could see from her eyes she was having an argument with herself.

"Please. You said yourself my mum's hurt because of them. I want to see this witch defeated. I've got to help – if it could bring Mum back."

Amelia sighed. "I'll come for you at midnight," she said at last. "Be ready."

When Kirby left the farm he went to the beach at Ruby Cove, to gather his thoughts and calm down a bit before heading home to Dad. The last thing he needed was for Dad to figure out he was up to something. The red cliffs were baking in the late-morning heat and the sand was frying-pan hot. He watched a few older boys playing beach football, laughing and yelling and having fun.

*They haven't got a clue*, Kirby thought. *They don't know what's out there.*

He wandered out to the smooth wet sand, picked up a few flat stones and began skimming them across the surface of the sea. Mum was the stone-skimming champion in the Simpson house.

As Kirby watched his stone bouncing one, two, three times on the water, he clung to the hope that if he could help Amelia get rid of the darkness infecting Craghaven, it might be enough to wake up Mum.

After a while he walked back up the steps to the harbour, where the warm salty air was filled with the clangs and rattles of workmen repairing the harbour wall.

"Kirby!" Dad was down on the water, showing another man around his lobster boat. "Alright, pal? You were up and out early this morning. Where'd you get to?"

"Just felt like a walk."

"This is Pete. You know old Terry MacLeod? Pete's his nephew. Terry's been taking him out on his boat, teaching him the ropes for a while now. Pete answered my advert. He's gonnae take over from me for a few weeks. You're gonnae catch lots and lots of lobster, aren't you, Pete?" He patted Pete on his huge back, and Pete laughed.

"Aye. I'm sure gonnae try," he said.

Dad climbed out of the boat and up the ladder to the harbour. He smelled of the sea.

"I'm sorry about yesterday," said Kirby. "I shouldn't have shouted at you."

Dad nodded. "It's fine, pal. Forget it. We're all feeling stressed just now."

"It's not fine." Kirby looked at the ground, shook his head. "I just get angry."

Down in the boat, Pete was making himself busy, very obviously trying not to listen.

"I know," said Dad. "I get angry too. There's not a second goes by I don't wish it was me in that bed instead of Mum."

"It shouldn't be anyone," said Kirby. The anger came again, flowing through him like molten metal in his veins. Because he knew the truth: he knew that the storm had not been a random act of nature. Someone had brought it to Craghaven – someone… or something.

"You OK?" asked Dad.

"Yeah." Kirby looked out over the bay towards Ruby Island, which stood alone in the North Sea, adrift and cut off from the world. "Just thinking of Mum again."

"Me too," said Dad. "Every single minute."

Out on Ruby Island, among the long grass, there stood a circle of standing stones.

The stones had been there for thousands of years.

Scientific papers had been written about them, and many experts argued about their purpose and meaning, though none of them knew the truth.

Brothers Swan and Swift knew.

At precisely the moment that Kirby was gazing out at the island from the harbour in Craghaven, Swan and Swift stood in the centre of the stone circle, their long black coats fluttering in the wind. They each held a bucket in one hand and a large paintbrush in the other, and as they glanced around at the tall stones they smiled.

"How this place brings back memories..." Brother Swift's straggly black hair whipped about his head in the sea breeze. "Of little people trying to please their gods with sacrifices and magic rituals. Not knowing that places like this belonged to Mother. Oh, how they fed her power..."

"And those times will come again, dear brother. The Shadowsmith has taken the bait. We'll soon reel her in."

Brother Swift gave a nod. "Our witches should be strong enough now. It's time."

"It is. And all the wars of the past will seem like an appetiser compared with what's to come when we are reunited. Shall we begin?"

"Let's."

They walked towards the stones, smiling, and put their buckets down on the grass. Each was filled with red liquid, into which they dipped their paintbrushes and began to paint the stones. As they worked, they sang, over and over again:

*Under the stars in the midnight-stained sky,*
*Unto the stones do they gather and cry.*
*The knife and the sword and the cup they do bring,*
*And they offer their life and their soul as they sing.*
*O darkness, O shadow, O Mother of Night,*
*Grant us protection with infinite might.*
*If enemies march strike them down in the mud.*
*Steal their minds and their hearts, their eyes and their blood.*

# Into the Woods

Kirby and Dad went to see Mum in the afternoon. Kirby finished reading *The Jungle Book* just before visiting time was up. It seemed to him as he read aloud that Dad was actually paying attention to the words. He still had his newspaper perched in his lap, of course, but he was looking up from the pages quite regularly.

They ate in Frankie's Café on the harbour as a special treat. Kirby had a bacon cheeseburger and Dad ordered Frankie's All Day Big Breakfast, which seemed too big for any normal human to finish.

At home, Kirby spent the evening choosing the next book he'd read to Mum. It was a big decision. Eventually he went with the first *Harry Potter*, because it was still their favourite despite the fact they'd read it so much the pages were falling out. And for the first time he could ever remember, Kirby found himself thinking about Dad too, wondering what sort of story *he* might like to hear.

Kirby's eyes returned to the clock again and again. Every minute that passed took him closer to the woods, to another adventure with Amelia. Only this time he had some idea of what was waiting. And it wasn't anything good.

He lay in bed and thought of Mum, of her laugh and her smile, and when he fell asleep he dreamed he was with her, in front of the fire in the living room. They sat in comfortable silence, reading to the sound of the popping fire, and Kirby was so happy, so content that he could have floated out of his chair…

"Kirby!"

He was ripped from his dream. When he opened his eyes, Amelia's face was so close that their noses were touching.

"What are you *doing*?" he yelped, almost falling out of bed.

"Just watching you sleep."

"Why were you doing that? Who *does* that?"

"Were you dreaming?" she asked. "What was it like?"

Kirby rubbed his eyes. "What? It was a dream! It was... *dreamlike...*" He climbed out of bed, still wearing his jeans and jumper. "How did you even get in? If my dad wakes up we're both dead."

This made Amelia smile. "He's sleeping like a baby. He won't wake up."

"What did you do to him?"

"Oh. Nothing. Well. I mean nothing bad. He's having a *lovely* dream."

"You are seriously weird."

"Thank you," said Amelia. Her face became very serious. "Any sign of that spider?"

"Nope."

"Good." Amelia's eyes sparked green. "What we're about to do isn't going to be easy. It's not too late to change your mind. I won't think you're a coward."

"I'm not changing anything. If there's even the smallest chance we might be helping Mum—"

"Fine," Amelia cut him off, "let's be having you."

They snuck out of the house and through the silent winding streets of Craghaven. The sea air was warm and still.

"You're going the wrong way," Kirby whispered.

"No. There's something else we need to do first."

On they walked, to the old church at the back of town, and then into the grounds, to the overgrown graveyard.

"Why have we come here?" said Kirby. "You didn't mention anything about walking round a graveyard in the dead of night. It's creepy."

"You'd better toughen up – sharpish," Amelia sniped back. "I need to make sure of something."

He followed her among the crumbling tombstones, his clothes catching on weeds and thorns. His mind began to trick him; he imagined he could hear footsteps behind him, pictured shadows crouched behind graves.

A barely discernible path led them through a tangle of trees to a wild patch of ground. Amelia stopped. She looked around, and then Kirby heard her take a sharp breath.

"What is it?"

She moved forward slowly, bent over and pulled something from the earth. It was a candle, black, caked with hardened waxy drippings. There were two more nearby, spaced a metre or so apart.

The uneasy feeling in Kirby's chest grew. "What are those for?"

"They're part of a spell." She stared at the candle in her hand. "Old magic. Really old."

"Do they belong to the witches?"

"No. They belong to the people who brought the witches back."

Kirby frowned. "Back? From where?"

"From the dead," said Amelia. "Three candles means three witches. They must have been buried here."

Kirby took a step back, his stomach turning loops, his head feeling too light for his body. "They're ghosts?" Amelia shot him a dark look. "You never mentioned anything about ghosts. Why would anyone want to bring them back?"

Amelia stared at the candles. She seemed shaken by something, upset. "I have no idea." Something in her voice told Kirby she wasn't telling him the truth. But why would she lie to him? Before he could ask anything else she turned away and said, "Come on. We have a job to do."

Twenty minutes later they were back at the farm. The abandoned farmhouse was a ghostly shadow set against the glaring blackness of the woods.

"Stick close," said Amelia, "and nothing will happen to you. Ready?"

Kirby was not ready. He knew Amelia knew he was not ready.

"No," he said. "But let's get it over with."

So they walked together, the boy and the girl, into the woods.

Across the farm, Farmer Weir sat alone in his tractor under the star-filled sky. On one side he had a flask of coffee, on the other his shotgun.

He took a sip of the steaming coffee. It was very strong and very sweet. Strong enough, he hoped, to keep him awake through the night so he might catch whatever was messing up his sheep so badly. His family had worked the land for generations, but he had never seen or heard of anything that could mangle a sheep in such a way. Well, tonight would be the end of it. The gun would see to that.

Farmer Weir took another sip of coffee, completely unaware that two very tall, very thin figures had appeared beside his tractor.

Brother Swift stared into the tractor cabin. He ran a hand through his thin greasy hair. "He has a gun, Brother Swan!" he said in mock fear. "Whatever shall we do?"

Brother Swan twitched his large nose. "Why, I expect we should turn back right away and never bother him again." Irony dripped from every word.

Although the brothers Swan and Swift were no more than one metre away from Farmer Weir, he did not see them or hear them. He sipped at his coffee and let out a long, loud burp.

"Pardon," said Brother Swan. Then he reached

into the cabin and touched Farmer Weir on the back of the head. At once his chin dropped to his chest and he began to snore. "Oh dear. He's only gone and fallen asleep. Who shall ensure the safety of his poor flock now?"

"Let's pay them a visit," said Brother Swift.

They walked out into the field among the sheep, which began to *baa* nervously.

"Why can't we just use human blood?" Brother Swan's bald head glistened in the light of the moon. "It's much more fun to obtain. Sheep's bleating is so dull compared to the vibrant screams of the little people."

"Because if dead bodies began piling up all over a small seaside town such as this, I daresay it might attract attention. We must carry out our work quietly. There'll be time aplenty for human misery once our mission has been accomplished. One thing at a time, eh?"

"I suppose so." Brother Swan placed his long spindly hands together as if he was praying. "Oh, how wonderful it'll be to have Mother back and be strong again."

"One step at a time, Brother Swan. One step at a time."

In perfect synchronisation, the brothers turned, and smiled, and walked towards the sheep.

# The First Witch

As they walked slowly through the twisting maze of trees, Kirby looked up beyond the thick tangle of branches to fragments of clear night sky, which reminded him that the world was still out there, waiting for him to come back.

The air in the woods was sweet and heavy and warm. The only sounds were the snap of fallen branches underfoot and the occasional rustle of an animal in the dark. Kirby didn't speak to Amelia as they went; he could feel the air around her crackle in the same strange way it had when they'd gone after the spiders, and he knew she was somewhere else in her head, somewhere he was glad not to be.

It was difficult to judge how much time passed as they walked in the darkness, but after a while things began to change around them. Kirby's eyes had grown accustomed to the lack of light, and he noticed that the trees had become warped, their branches sharp and jagged.

A sudden flash of pain in his arm made him twist away. Had something stung him or bitten him?

"Let me see. Does it hurt?"

"Stings a bit."

Amelia rolled back his sleeve, examining his arm as best she could. Even in the gloom it was easy to see the long cut running down the inside of Kirby's forearm towards his wrist. She stared at the trees all around. "She's stronger than I thought."

"Who?"

"The witch. She's twisting this place around, using the woods as protection."

"Are you telling me," said Kirby in a panicked whisper, "that the *trees* are against us?"

"Yes," said Amelia. "I mean – you know – if we're lucky it'll just be the trees."

Something coiled around Kirby's ankle, pulled him to the damp woodland floor. Roots squirmed over him like snakes, wrapping around his arms and neck. He was overcome with panic. He tried to scream out, but there was no air in his lungs. As he kicked and fought, Kirby was distantly aware of Amelia standing over him, muttering in that strange language. The roots squeezed his neck, and he gasped and struggled. Amelia raised her voice and suddenly they loosened their grip. Cold, wonderful air rushed into Kirby's body. He clutched at his throat as Amelia pulled him to his feet with surprising strength.

She didn't speak. She only stared into his eyes. He understood at once, and nodded.

They began to run.

It was as if the woods had been sleeping, and had suddenly wakened. The trees were alive with movement, swaying and lashing like they were caught in the wind, and as Kirby and Amelia ran, branches whipped towards them. They ducked and dodged and spun, never letting go of each other.

Kirby didn't know where they were running to; he only knew that he had to keep moving, no matter how tired he became, no matter how his legs ached, or the trees would wrap around him and rip him apart.

They took a hard right turn, ducking under the swing of an incoming branch, jumping over the grasping tendrils of roots and weeds, and then everything fell silent and still.

They were standing in a circular clearing of sorts, with only a scattering of trees and a floor carpeted in thick moss. Above, the sky was open and endless. The night had been warm and pleasant, but now Kirby felt the air growing cold. The hair on his arms stood up, and the steam of his breath curled around him.

Amelia was still holding his hand. She gripped it tighter. "Stay close," she said. "She's here."

Kirby could see nothing but tree and shadow and sky. The place was so silent it made his ears ache. "Whereabouts?"

Amelia peered into the dark. "I'm working on that." She took a hesitant step forward, pulling Kirby with her. He kept thinking about the dead sheep in the field.

"When we find her, use the wand like you did against the spiders." And then Amelia froze.

Kirby followed her gaze to a spot just ahead where something was standing in their path. It looked, at first, like a ragged shadow. But it was darker than a shadow, just as the spiders had been. There was something vaguely human about it – arms and legs and a head – but the form was constantly changing, and the frayed edges of the silhouette fluttered like a flag in the wind. Kirby could make out no features, no face or eyes.

"You shouldn't have come here." Amelia's voice was loud and strong. "You know what has to happen now. I can't let you stay."

The shadow flickered and warped.

When the witch spoke, her voice tore the silence. "What do you care, little miss?" she said to Amelia. "Compared to the little people you're a god. You could have anything. Be anything. And yet you choose to defend 'em."

"I do." Amelia shifted her weight as if she was getting ready to make a move. "I've been to the graveyard where you slept. Someone brought you back. Who?"

The shadow flickered again. "You'll find out soon enough, girl."

Amelia took a half-step forward. "You're angry," she said, "with the world. I feel it."

"You'd be angry too if you were hunted and stoned to death. And all I ever tried to do was help 'em. I delivered their babies and washed their dead and treated their animals for disease. No more."

"The world has changed since then. Come with me. Let me take you back to the graveyard."

"I ent going back," said the witch. "I want to be free. They said for that to happen I have to take care of you, Shadowsmith."

Amelia tilted her head, frowned. "How do you know that word?"

The witch did not answer. A cold breeze filled the clearing, brushing Kirby's cheek, and the witch grew and changed shape, becoming an enormous black bear with glowing red eyes, still ragged at the edges.

Kirby's skin was covered in goosebumps, his scalp tingled. His heart beat hard and fast, and every muscle in his body seemed to quiver and shake.

"Kirby?" Amelia squeezed his hand, and he felt the warmth of her touch spreading up his arm, into his chest. He managed to turn his head away from the nightmarish bear and looked into her eyes, which were bright, almost sparkling. "Use the hazel," she said. And then she let go of his hand, and turned and walked towards the bear.

Kirby did as she asked. He found a spot beside a tree and drew a wide circle around himself.

Amelia strolled towards the witch, stopping only a few metres away. As a bear it towered over her, even on all fours. She looked like a doll next to it.

She looked up, directly into the witch's eyes. "I'll ask you one more time. Who brought you back?"

The bear growled, and the growl sounded like a laugh.

"I'm sorry," said Amelia, "but you brought this on yourself."

The great bear threw its head back and roared, shaking the branches of the trees. Then it leapt forward and crashed into Amelia, sending her flying backwards and landing with a heavy thud on the woodland floor.

The witch stood over her, standing on its hind legs, staring down with blood-red eyes.

Kirby cried out to Amelia. He thought she was dead.

But Amelia Pigeon was not dead. She got up, dusted herself off and said, "That wasn't very nice."

The bear-witch made to swipe at her with a huge black paw, but Amelia raised her hazel wand and began to speak. The bear's paw froze in the air.

From the safety of his circle, Kirby listened and Amelia's words wrapped around him, warmed him, filled his head and his heart.

The bear was struggling against Amelia, the rough edge of its body strobing in the shadow. It roared and backed away, pacing in a circle.

"If you'd stop trying to kill me this would be over much quicker." Amelia's yellow raincoat shone in the moonlight.

Just like that, the bear flickered and became human-shaped again, wrapped in rags of darkest black. The witch began to speak.

Whenever Amelia spoke her magical language, it felt shining and wondrous. When the witch spoke the same language, her words cut the air like rusted blades. Where Amelia's voice brought hope, the hag's brought fear. Kirby covered his ears, but the sound was still there, in his head. He began to shake, felt like the world was closing in around him.

Amelia stumbled back, shaking cobwebs from her mind.

The witch advanced, still chanting her awful words, and Amelia backed away until she was pressed against a tree. The witch was close to her now, and with every step her voice grew louder and the darkness grew deeper.

Amelia dropped to her knees.

"Amelia!" yelled Kirby.

But Amelia was not done. Still on her knees, looking at the ground with her hair hanging over her face, she burst upward. For a moment the darkness lit up, alive with fiery golden light, and then it descended again.

Amelia was back on her knees, panting, but her burst of magic had thrown the witch across the clearing, where she was picking herself slowly off the woodland floor. Then the witch was the great black bear again, charging across the clearing towards Amelia, who was still looking at the ground, seemingly oblivious.

Kirby moved without thinking, more on instinct than anything else, outside of his safe circle, holding the hazel wand high. "Oi!" he said.

The bear stopped in its tracks and turned to face him, and in that moment Kirby wondered what on earth he was doing.

The bear charged at him, and before he'd even thought about drawing another circle of protection, a great paw had knocked the hazel from his hand, sending him tumbling to the ground. He rolled away, avoiding the hulking body as it tried to crush him. Then he was on his feet, running, scrambling, climbing the nearest tree.

Below, the bear crashed against the trunk, uprooting it, tipping it over with Kirby holding tight among the leaves. He clung on as well as he could, but the assault was relentless. The bear thrashed at the tree, breaking thick branches like they were twigs, teeth flashing, coming closer and closer...

Then it reared back, its eyes rolling, and it moaned in pain.

Kirby saw Amelia standing behind the bear, fury burning in her eyes. It became the witch again, but her shape was loose and sketchy, and as Amelia spoke the witch grabbed at the branches and swiped at the air.

Kirby saw that the fallen tree itself was moving about him, the branches twining around the witch, wrapping and squeezing. She changed shape in desperation, to a bear once more, but she was too weak to resist Amelia's magic. The bark began to grow over the bear-witch, encasing her – first her legs, then her arms and body, until only her head remained. Her eyes were wide in horror as it crept slowly up her neck, over the back of her head, her face and eyes and snout, until, at last, the great black bear was gone and Kirby could hear nothing but silence and the sound of his breathing.

Amelia came over, grabbed his hand, and pulled him from the tangled grasp of the branches to standing. "You OK?"

Kirby could not speak; he was too stunned. He nodded.

"Good," said Amelia. Then she punched him on the arm.

"Ow! What's that for?"

"For being thick!" she yelled and punched him again.

"Ow! Will you stop doing that!"

"I told you to stay put!"

"She was going to kill you!"

"I had it under control!"

"Didn't look that way to me!"

"Oh," said Amelia, "I'm sorry! I keep forgetting you're a master at hunting the forces of darkness! If you'd been killed..." She stopped then, and Kirby thought for a moment that she was going to punch him again. He braced himself. But Amelia didn't punch him. She hugged him. "Don't do that again," she said. "Next time, do as I say."

Kirby smiled. "So I get to come along next time?"

Amelia didn't answer. She shook her head, and huffed, and stormed off through the woods.

Kirby had one last look at the tree, touching the part that had been the bear. Then he ran after her, back towards the farm, and the world he knew.

# Grounded

The woods had returned to normal. There were no angry, thrashing branches or grabbing, snaking roots. The trees were just trees.

As they headed back towards the farmhouse, Amelia slowed and started to sway, and by the time they had reached the border of the woodland and the farm, Kirby was helping her to walk.

"I'm fine," she insisted, though her voice was weak. "I'm just tired. It's not an easy business, getting rid of a witch. I need to sleep, that's all."

"That witch called you something... Shadowsmith. What's that?"

"An old word," said Amelia. "She shouldn't have known it."

Kirby helped her into the farmhouse ruin, and was amazed again at how cosy and comfortable it was inside, with a fire burning in the fireplace.

Amelia lay down on the couch and yawned. "You should go home."

"OK, I'll check in on you tomorrow. Y' know, just to make sure."

Her eyes were closed, but she smiled. "I'll be sleeping for a little longer than that."

"Oh. How long?"

"Don't know." Her voice was far away now, at the edge of sleep. "I'll come for you when I wake." Her head lolled to one side, and she breathed deeply and rhythmically.

Kirby took a blanket from an old rocking chair in the corner and covered Amelia. Then, with nothing else to do, he left the farmhouse, closing the door gently, although he was sure that even if he'd slammed it as hard as he could it would not have woken her. He began to walk away, but something stopped him – a curious feeling, a hunch.

Kirby returned to the door, reached for the handle and opened it.

This time there were no lights inside, no cosy kitchen, no fire warming the room. No Amelia. Everything was bare and cold and black, as dead on the inside as it looked from the outside.

On the walk home Kirby listened to the sound of the sea, watched feathers of cloud pass across the moon, and thought of the witch in the forest, trapped forever in a tree – thanks, in very small part, to him.

It seemed that the world was a little safer.

Most importantly, now that the first witch was gone, Kirby could hope Mum was a little closer to waking up.

When he reached his house, he opened the front door, tiptoed through to the kitchen and poured himself a glass of milk. He was thirsty.

"Where have you been?"

Dad was sitting at the kitchen table in his dressing gown in the dark. When Kirby heard his voice, he was so shocked he blew milk out of his nose. The light from the fridge painted half of Dad's face. He did not look happy.

"Sit. Down."

Kirby sat. The milk was swirling around in his belly and his hands were clammy.

"Well? Where were you?"

"Just out," said Kirby meekly.

"Out where?"

"Just for a walk."

"A walk?" Kirby could tell Dad was trying not to

lose the plot. "In the middle of the night? Are you insane?"

"I'm sorry." Kirby's mind was racing. It seemed like Amelia had put Dad under a spell earlier, so that she and Kirby could sneak out. He reckoned the spell must have worn off when Amelia went to sleep back at the farmhouse.

"Sorry?" yelled Dad. "That's it?"

"I didn't mean any harm."

"You're twelve years old! You don't go out for a walk in the dead of night! Do you not think I've got enough on my plate right now without you adding to my troubles?"

Kirby looked up from the table, anger prickling the back of his neck. "Oh, so that's all I am, is it? A bother? A nuisance?"

Dad shook his head. "Don't twist my words, pal. You know what I meant."

"Yeah," said Kirby, "I do know. You wish you didn't have to worry about me. Maybe I should have just kept on walking and never come back."

Dad banged his fist on the table, making Kirby jump. "You think that would help? Eh? You think I want to lose you as well as your mum? Get up to your room. I don't even want to look at you right now."

Kirby opened his mouth, but he didn't know what

to say. He knew he'd gone too far. He wished he could tell Dad the truth: that the only reason he'd snuck out was because he wanted to help Mum. But he knew how ridiculous it would sound if he started going on about witches and magic. It would only make things worse. He got up from the table and moved towards the door.

"I'm sorry," he said.

"You're also grounded," said Dad. "One week."

Kirby didn't answer. He shut the kitchen door and left Dad alone in silence.

In the clearing in the woods, Brothers Swan and Swift stood over the fallen tree, staring down at the twisted trunk in which Amelia had trapped the witch's soul. On the ground by their feet sat two buckets. In each bucket was a tangled collection of slimy creatures.

"Well," said Brother Swift, "it's not how I would choose to go."

"No," said Brother Swan, "nor me. If you listen close... I think you can still hear her screaming in there."

The part of the tree that had once been a witch still resembled a bear, but only if you looked carefully. Brother Swan patted what had been the witch-bear's snout. "The girl's still strong. This is proper Shadowsmith magic."

Brother Swift blew his long black hair from his eyes. "I don't think we ought to be too worried. She's nothing compared to what she used to be. That business with Mother took a lot out of her. She's ripe for the picking, dear brother, you mark my words."

"And the boy?" said Brother Swan. "What d'you think she has planned for him?"

"Who can tell? But let's keep a watch on him. There may come a time when he's useful."

They picked up their buckets. The black things inside writhed.

Brother Swan patted the witch's snout again. "Oh well, you played your part," he said. "No rest for the wicked, dear."

And then the clearing was empty once more.

# The Mist

Over the next week, Kirby was only allowed to leave the house when they visited Mum in hospital. He had hoped there would be some change in her now that the first witch was gone – a blink of an eye or a twitch of a finger – but her condition was just the same. Every day Kirby would sit in the little private room and read *Harry Potter* aloud, and he began to notice that although Dad sat with his newspaper open on his lap, he no longer flipped through the pages. He was listening to the story. Really listening. And that made Kirby want to read and read and read.

They barely spoke a word to each other all week. Kirby wanted to explain. He wanted to tell Dad about Amelia and the dangerous adventures they'd shared and why he'd snuck out. But he didn't.

On the silent drive home over the coastal road on Thursday afternoon they saw heavy clouds rolling over the North Sea towards Craghaven, and a thick mist breathing inland. Ruby Island, which sat on the horizon like a wedge of cheese, was swallowed, and before long the mist and rain had reached the village.

When the car pulled up outside their house, Dad turned in his seat and said, "Right then. That's been a week. You can go out if you want."

Kirby put on his raincoat and went for a walk. He was hoping that he'd turn a corner and find Amelia smiling at him in the rain, but she was nowhere to be seen.

Down at the harbour, the tide was out. The ghostly shapes of the beached fishing boats looked spooky in the mist, and the irregular rocks of the storm-damaged harbour wall jutted up like rotten teeth.

And then, down on the wet sand, Kirby saw a flash of yellow, and his heart leapt. "Amelia?" he yelled. "Amelia! Up here!"

The yellow raincoat came closer, and beside it was another raincoat, this one dark blue, much more difficult to spot through the fog.

"Kirby? That you?"

The voice wasn't Amelia's, and when Kirby realised he wouldn't be seeing her, the hope and excitement rushed out of him. Two faces peered up at him. Charlie Hunter and Ewan Marshall were in Kirby's class.

"Who's Amelia?" asked Charlie.

"She your girlfriend?" added Ewan.

"Ha! Good one," said Kirby. "Just someone my dad knows. What you up to?"

"Looking for crabs."

"Caught any?"

"Nah. Think we'll head over to the rocks at Ruby Cove."

"Yeah," said Kirby. "Good luck."

The two boys began to walk away but Charlie turned back. Kirby could no longer make out his face through the rain and mist.

"I heard about your mum," he said. "Is she going to be OK?"

"We don't know yet."

"I hope she gets better," said Ewan.

"Thanks."

As Charlie and Ewan disappeared into the fog, Kirby sat down on the wet harbour wall, his legs dangling over the edge. He wasn't surprised the boys hadn't invited him to go crab fishing.

It was the same at school every lunchtime or break. It wasn't that the other kids disliked him. Not at all. They were pleasant to him. They would talk to him. But they wouldn't invite him to sit at their table for lunch, or to their sleepovers or birthday parties. Kirby felt like there was an invisible barrier between him and the others, always had been, something that made him a little different.

He supposed that's why Amelia had found him. But really, who could tell what was going on inside that curly-thatched head of hers? He'd never met anyone like her, and he still wasn't sure whether that was a good or bad thing.

"You OK, pal?"

The sudden sound of Dad's voice almost made Kirby slip over the edge.

"I will be when I get over the heart attack."

Dad smiled. Kirby got to his feet and they stood in awkward silence for a long moment, listening to the patter of the rain on the water.

"Eh, I'm going to repair some creels," said Dad. "Could you help?"

Dad's creels were stacked up on the harbour wall beside his boat. He took four of them down, turning them over in his big arms, and put them on the ground. "Hold this still, will you?"

Kirby held the creel while his dad took what looked like a big knitting needle and began to sew a hole in the net back together. His movements were smooth, his hands delicate. He glanced at Kirby through the rain. “Sure you’re OK?”

Kirby nodded. Then he said, “I’m really sorry about the other night. I mean it.”

Dad nodded back. “I know. And I’m sorry for shouting the way I did. You scared me, Kirby.”

“I didn’t mean to.”

“Look,” said Dad, “we’re both under a lot of stress. We’re dealing with some big stuff. I understand why you felt like you had to get away, I do. But when I woke up and found your bed empty I thought I’d lost you. Don’t do that to me again, pal.”

Kirby stared at his shoes. “I won’t.”

They stood in silence again. The rain grew heavier.

“Did you have lots of friends when you were at school?” asked Kirby.

Dad closed the first hole in the creel net and moved to the next. “You shouldn’t worry about things like that. There’s plenty of time...”

“You didn’t answer my question.”

“Believe it or not,” said Dad, “I was a lot like you.”

Kirby narrowed his eyes. "You? You were like me?"

"Don't sound so surprised!"

"I just mean… we're not exactly alike now, are we?"

Kirby saw the smile on his dad's lips fade, and he wished he could learn not to throw his words around so carelessly.

"I've never been one for reading," said Dad. "Fishing was always my thing."

"Fishing?" said Kirby. "You? Never!"

This brought the smile back to Dad's face. "I know, shocking, eh? But the reason I fished so much, apart from loving it, was that I could be alone without feeling lonely. See, I didn't have many friends. Didn't have any, as a matter of fact. Never knew what to say to people. So I spent a lot of time on my own. But when I was fishing, I felt part of something bigger. Still do."

Kirby stared up at his dad. He'd never heard him speaking this way. He supposed he'd always thought of him as being like the rocks around Craghaven: unbreakable, able to stand up to anything.

"How you feel when you fish," he said, "sounds just how I feel when I read. I'm not lonely when

I'm in a book."

"I know," said Dad. "We've always known, Mum and me." He finished repairing the creel and moved on to the next one, effortlessly threading the needle through the net, pulling the two open ends back together. "There were a lot of times I should have spoken to you," he said, "and a lot of times I wanted to. I just never knew what to say. I'm not good with words."

"You're doing pretty well now."

"All those times when I was your age I wished I could change... become someone else. But look at me now. I've got Mum, and you, and I wouldn't change that for all the fish in the sea. So don't you bother your head about it, pal. Friends will come in time. Just you be you. The rest will sort itself out." He finished repairing the final creel and stacked it with the others.

"Mum's going to be OK, Dad," said Kirby. "I feel it. She'll come back to us."

"I feel it too." Dad frowned, looking out over the mist-cloaked harbour towards the sea. The swell was growing, the waves capped with clouds of tumbling white foam. "Weather's gone loopy," he said, scratching his beard.

"Yeah," said Kirby, "it has a bit." And in his head

he wondered where Amelia was, and he wished she would come back soon. Because another storm was coming, and who knew what it would bring.

# THREE

# The Fairground

# Fortune-teller

The fairground arrived the next day, a jumble of lorries and caravans appearing from the mist and setting up in a field just outside of town. Kirby walked out to watch them build their stalls and rides. If anything the fog was getting thicker, and the touch of it, cold and damp against his skin, made him uneasy. The shouts of the fairground folk pierced the air as they worked, hammering and clanging, and before long many of the rides were up, including a huge Ferris wheel that Kirby longed to try.

He left the field and went home, finding Dad in the kitchen and an overpowering stench of garlic in the air. "Thought I'd give spag-bol a go," he said, stirring the contents of a simmering pot, "seeing as it's Thursday. Mum always does spag-bol on Thursdays."

Kirby leaned over the cooker, inspecting the thick brownish gloop in the pot. It bubbled angrily at him. "Looks interesting," he said. "Mum's isn't usually that colour though, is it?"

"Hmm. I was wondering about that as well. Where've you been, anyway?"

Kirby told him about the fairground. "So can we go?"

Dad stirred the pot again, and brought out the wooden spoon, staring at the steaming lump on the end. He popped it into his mouth, chewed, grimaced as if Kirby had kicked him on the shin, and said, "Good idea. I haven't been to the carnival for years." Then he tossed the wooden spoon back in the pot and switched off the cooker. "I'll buy us fish and chips for dinner on the way."

Even in the thick mist the carnival was alive with light and colour. Fairgrounds didn't often make it as far along the east coast as Craghaven, so the entire town was buzzing, and the place was crowded despite the weather.

Kirby was first in line for a go on the big wheel. The glow from the fairground lights lit up the fog, turning it into a fluorescent sea, and when he was up on the wheel, Kirby felt like he was Peter Pan floating through the enchanted sky towards Neverland.

He won a water pistol on the coconut shy, terrorised his dad on the bumper cars, and ate candyfloss until he felt sick. Dad had a go on the strongman hammer. Then another. And another, until he was so exhausted from trying to ring the bell that the owner of the stall had to give him a drink of water.

"It must be rigged." He rubbed his shoulder as they walked away. "Right, I think that's enough for one night. Home, eh?"

They were almost out of the field when Kirby spotted a small, shabby tent almost hidden away among the bright rides and stalls. There was nothing fancy about it, only red and white striped canvas, an entrance covered by a curtain of beads and a small sign that read:

"I've always wanted to have my fortune told," said Kirby. "Can I, Dad?"

Dad squinted at the tent. "Really? It's all rubbish."

"It's just a bit of fun."

Dad reached into his pocket and gave Kirby a few coins. "Go for it," he said. "I'll wait here."

Kirby swept through the curtain into a tiny square space lit by the glow of many fairy lights strung around the red-striped walls. There was a little round table with a chair on either side. One of the chairs was empty. In the other sat an old woman dressed completely in black, wearing a floppy hat that was too big for her. She kept readjusting it. She smiled up at Kirby, and her face was nothing more than a collection of wrinkles and two shining black eyes.

"Welcome, boy," she said. "Cross my palm with silver."

"I've got two pounds," said Kirby. "Will that do?"

"Hand it over."

Kirby did as she asked.

"Sit," she said.

Kirby sat on the chair and stared across the table.

The old woman pursed her lips and held out a hand. "Give us your hand."

She took Kirby's hand and studied it, palm up, a look of deep concentration on her face. Then, suddenly, she let it go, recoiling from him as if he had stung her. Her wrinkles gathered into a sad, concerned look, and she said, “You’re going to lose her.”

The lights and sounds of the fairground seemed so very far away inside the little tent. Kirby stared at the fortune-teller. His heart quickened. “What did you say?”

“I’m so sorry, so very, very sorry. I can’t help what I see...”

“What *did* you see?” asked Kirby.

“There’s someone close to you,” she said. “Someone very close. A female. I see her lying down. And when I look a little further ahead she’s gone... empty.”

Kirby felt like someone had reached in and grabbed his heart with icy hands. She was talking about Mum. She had to be.

He stood up, numb. “I have to go.” Then he was out of the tent, back among the chaos of the carnival, and it seemed like the world was moving past him in a blur.

“You alright?” said Dad.

“Mmm?”

“I said, are you alright? You look frightened half to death. What did that fortune-teller say to you?”

“Oh, nothing much. Just a lot of rubbish like you said. Waste of money really.”

But the fortune-teller's words haunted him. All the way home, and through a sleepless night, he could hear her voice: *You're going to lose her.*

# Taken

The usual smell of burnt toast greeted Kirby when he made his way down to the kitchen next morning. Dad was sitting at the table reading the paper with a steaming coffee, a deep frown on his brow.

"Something up?" Kirby asked.

"Mmm? Oh. Paper says a local boy's missing."

"Missing?"

"Yeah. His parents lost him at the carnival last night. He's only six."

Kirby straightened up in his seat. He had that strange sinking feeling in his stomach, the one that the spiders gave him, the witch in the woods too. "Can I see the paper after you?"

Dad nodded, and handed the newspaper over. Kirby read the story from start to finish. The young boy's name was Charlie Grant. Kirby recognised the photo – one of the little ones at his old primary school.

The newspaper report was implying as strongly as it could that someone had snatched him at the carnival. Kirby suspected they were right. Charlie had been taken. But not necessarily by a person.

When he was dressed, Kirby walked back up through town to the field where the carnival was set up. There were police everywhere. The entrance was taped off. As he approached, a policewoman said, "Can't go in there, son."

Kirby walked away, hands in pockets, and watched the comings and goings from a spot on an old stone wall at the edge of the field.

"Well, this isn't good, is it?" said a voice.

Amelia was beside him, perched on the wall in her yellow raincoat and Wellingtons, swinging her legs.

Kirby blinked to make sure she was really there. "You're OK!" He climbed down and looked at her.

"Of course I'm OK." Amelia rolled her eyes. "As if I wouldn't be OK!"

Kirby folded his arms. "Well thanks for letting me know! I was grounded for a week because of you!"

"Me? What did I do?" Kirby was about to answer when Amelia said, "Hold that thought..."

She stepped back, looking the wall up and down. It was old, built from many stones all wedged together with dark gaps in between them. Amelia reached into one of the gaps, her tongue stuck to her top lip in concentration, and she shuffled her arm about. When she pulled her hand out, she was holding something about the size of a mouse, something black and wriggling. She dropped it to the ground, raised a foot, and brought her Wellington down hard. The thing, whatever it was, exploded under her boot, leaving a smear of black goo on the grass. Kirby pinched his nose. It smelled like rotting seaweed.

"What," he said, "was that?"

Amelia shrugged. "It's like I said before. When the witches came through, so did some other stuff. Pests. Vermin. No big deal."

"Oh, more good news then."

"What's wrong with you?" Amelia asked. "Did you miss your nap today?"

"When I got home after you beat the witch, Dad was awake. He was out of his mind. Grounded me for a week. You dropped me in it!"

Amelia raised her hands. "Relax," she said. "Freeze out."

"Freeze out... you mean *chill* out?"

"Possibly. I'm no good with your jargon. Look, next time we'll get you home before I fall asleep. That way your dad will definitely still be under the spell. OK?"

'OK," Kirby muttered. He was so pleased to see Amelia again, he couldn't stay angry with her for long. And they needed to start searching for wee Charlie.

"In the meantime," said Amelia, "we've more important things to worry about." She nodded towards the fairground, where the police were buzzing around. "They do a good job of looking busy, don't they?" Then her eyes widened, and she looked around. "It's foggy!"

"Oh, good spot."

"I haven't been awake for long. Bit slow when I first get up. How long has the mist been here?"

"Since a few days after you took care of the witch in the woods."

Amelia stuck her tongue out, tasted the air. She pursed her lips. "Told you one of them is good with weather. She'll be the one who caused the storm." She paused, and her face softened. "How is your mum by the way?"

"The same," said Kirby sadly. "Amelia... you don't think... well, when we got rid of the first witch, you don't think we made the others angry, do you?

I mean, the mist appeared really soon after. And then this boy was snatched..."

Amelia thought about this.

"Nah, ghosts don't usually work together. They know I'm here, though. It's probably rattled them a bit."

"But why take the boy?"

"Bait," said Amelia. "This one's smart. She knows I'll come after her, but with a little boy in the equation, I'll have to be careful, make sure he doesn't come to any harm."

"So how do we find her? And how do we stop her?"

Amelia gave him a grim smile. "Well, as far as finding her goes, we won't need to look far." She pointed to the carnival. "She's in there somewhere."

Out on lonely Ruby Island, Brothers Swan and Swift sat side by side in the circle of standing stones. Between them were two buckets, each filled to bursting with skittering creatures, all legs and slime and pincers.

"Looks like it's about to kick off over there." Brother Swan nodded towards the mainland.

He reached into one of the buckets, picking out a many-legged creature, and examined it. Then he popped it, writhing and hissing, into his mouth, and bit it in half. When he chewed, black liquid ran from the corner of his lips. The part of the creature that was still in his hand continued to wriggle. "She's about to go after our second witch."

Brother Swift nodded, and selected his own oily black snack from the bucket, picking off a pair of sharp claws before jamming the creature into his mouth.

"Should be an interesting fight," he said, through a gob full of half-chewed bug. "Our witch has kidnapped a boy. She means business."

"They always do." Brother Swan smacked his lips. "And then they meet the Shadowsmith." Silence for a moment, until he said, "Shall we go and watch?"

"Champion idea."

There was a swirl of mist, and the circle of standing stones was empty.

# Skeletons

"What do we do?" said Kirby, staring into the quiet fairground.

"We have a nosy," said Amelia. "See what we can see. Come on."

She moved towards a gap in the dyke that served as the carnival entrance.

"Can't go that way." Kirby caught her up. He nodded to the policewoman standing guard. "She won't let us in."

Amelia gave him a funny look, like he'd just said something ridiculous. "Just come on."

As they approached the policewoman, she stared down at them. Amelia gave her a smile. "Hello," she said brightly.

"Hello," the policewoman replied, returning Amelia's smile with an absent-minded one of her own. She stepped aside and let Amelia and Kirby pass, and then went back to guarding the gate.

"How did you do that?" Kirby whispered.

Amelia touched the side of her nose.

"I'd do that all the time if I could," said Kirby. "I could go to the cinema and see all the films I'm not allowed to see! Can we do that one day?"

"Nope."

Kirby kicked a stone. He didn't understand girls at all.

Amelia was no longer paying attention to him. She was staring around, sniffing the air, touching things. They wandered all the way round the carnival, through the rides, between the stalls and among the maze of caravans and trucks. The place was quiet, save for the occasional police officer or carnival hand.

"She's hidden well." Amelia scrunched up her nose.

"You sure the witch is here?"

"Definitely. I can feel her. But her signal is weak. She knows we're here and she's hiding as best she can. We'll have to come back later. Tonight. They usually come out to play at night."

A stabbing pain ran through Kirby's hand then, where the spider had burst through the flesh. He cringed, stepped back, and thought he caught sight of something, a shadow in the mist, but it was gone as quick as he could blink.

"What's wrong?" said Amelia. "Is it your hand? Let me see." She took his hand and examined it. Then she looked around the carnival, worry in her eyes.

"What's wrong?"

"Oh... nothing. It's just a feeling I have, that's all. I'm sure it's fine." She shook it off and smiled, but Kirby could tell she was putting the smile on just for him. "Come on, then," she said.

Back through the thick mist they went, towards the road, when Amelia stopped. "Oho! Look at that. A fortune-teller!" She pointed to a tent Kirby barely recognised in the pale, fog-smothered world.

Kirby frowned. "Aye. I went to see her last night."

"You never did!" Amelia shot him a scornful look. "Kirby Simpson, I thought I'd taught you better than that! These people are frauds! Clueless imposters! Do you know how difficult it is to see the future? Even for me! I can't see anything other than a few jumbled tomorrows and maybes."

When she said that Kirby smiled a proper smile for the first time since he'd visited the fortune-teller. Her words had been playing on his mind from the moment he left her tent.

"She's really a fake?"

"Of course she is? Why? What's wrong? What did she say to you?"

Kirby looked at his feet. He was embarrassed he'd let the old woman frighten him.

"She told me... she said I was going to lose someone close to me. It didn't take a genius to work out she meant Mum."

For a second he thought Amelia was going to hug him. But she held back and said, "Oh, Kirby! Of all the mean-hearted, hurtful things to tell you! We can't let her get away with this. In fact..." She didn't finish her sentence. She turned and marched off towards the tent.

"Oh no," said Kirby. "Don't do anything stupid!"

She disappeared through the curtain of beads, and the next moment an ear-splitting shriek burst from the tent.

Kirby looked around, panicked, expecting police officers to come swarming all over them at any moment. They didn't. It seemed they hadn't heard the commotion. Or Amelia hadn't let them. Kirby sped towards the tent and brushed through the entrance.

Amelia was standing in the middle of the small square space, her arms folded, staring at the fortune-teller, who was backed against the other side looking terrified out of her wits. She was holding her hands out, her two index fingers making the sign of a cross.

"Demon!" she was yelling. "Monster!"

To which Amelia replied, "Oh for goodness' sake sit down, you stupid old bag of bones."

But the woman did not sit down. She seemed genuinely horrified by Amelia. "Be gone! Be gone, you spectre!"

Amelia turned to Kirby and rolled her eyes. "She's a decent actress, I'll give her that." Then she turned back to the fortune-teller and said, "My friend here tells me you've been scaring him by saying despicable things about his future. I want you to tell him you're a fraud and none of it meant anything. Tell him he isn't going to lose anyone."

The fortune-teller stared wide-eyed at Amelia. "I cannot take back what I have seen," she said. "Just as you cannot take back the wickedness in your past."

It was as if her words had knocked the wind from Amelia.

"I know what you are," said the fortune-teller, her twinkling little dark eyes all screwed up. "I know where you've been. I know what you're capable of."

Amelia swayed on the spot. "Kirby, let's go."

"So many bad deeds," the fortune-teller went on. "Such a dark heart. Monster! Get out of my tent!"

Amelia grabbed Kirby by the arm and dragged him away from the darkness inside, back to the misty world of the carnival. She was breathless and shaken. Kirby had never seen her like this, not even when she was facing a witch. A thought hit him.

"*She's* not the witch, is she, that loony?"

Amelia shook her head. "She's nothing but an old woman messing in things she doesn't understand."

"The stuff she was saying about you!" said Kirby with a nervous laugh. "What a load of rubbish! You're not a monster. You haven't done anything wrong..."

Amelia looked right into his eyes, the green of her own burning bright.

"Everyone has a skeleton or two in their cupboard," she said. Then she turned and walked away.

# Hide and Seek

Midnight. The witching hour.

Amelia had somehow snuck into the house again, and she stood in Kirby's room and watched him tie the laces on his trainers. When he stood up, Kirby sighed.

"What's up?" Amelia said.

Since he left Amelia earlier that day, Kirby had been wondering what kind of terrifying skeletons she might have trapped in her closet. It seemed like she was hiding things from her past. Things she was ashamed of maybe. But he couldn't ask her. He daren't. So he said, "I feel a bit bad sneaking out again after last time. I promised Dad..."

"Come with me." Amelia beckoned him towards Dad's bedroom.

He was lying on his back, flat out, with his mouth open. She reached into her yellow raincoat and brought out her hazel twig. She pressed the tip of the wand gently against Dad's forehead and he smiled a dopey smile and said, in a faraway voice, "More bacon please, Mummy." Kirby sniggered.

"There," said Amelia, "he's dreaming. This time we'll get you home before he wakes up. I promise."

The fairground seemed like a different place under the cloak of midnight. Moonlight fought its way through the thick mist, falling on the towering shapes of the carnival rides. There was an eerie silence to the place, an emptiness that seemed unnatural.

"Feel anything?" Kirby said in a hushed tone.

"Not much." Amelia was a few paces in front, walking slowly, sniffing the air, considering her every step. "She's in the background, like static."

"Is she making this mist?" Kirby swiped a hand through the air. "I wish it would clear off, it makes my skin crawl."

"I don't think weather's her thing. This one likes playing games."

"Will she hurt Charlie?"

Amelia turned to face him. "One thing at a time."

On they went, through the creeping blackness, until they had covered the entirety of the fairground, from the rides and stalls to the maze of caravans and trucks.

"Are you *sure* she's here?" Kirby was cold, and tired, and cranky.

"Are you an expert all of a sudden?" Amelia snapped.

"You don't need to be like that."

"What I need is to concentrate. What I *need* is to not have you rabbiting on in my ear."

"Are you here about the boy?" said a third voice.

They turned slowly, to see a girl standing in the open doorway of one of the caravans. She was smaller than Kirby, but also older – maybe thirteen or fourteen – and she wore a dressing gown and slippers.

"Hello," said Amelia. "What's your name?"

"Lizzie," said the girl.

Amelia gave Lizzie one of her sparkling smiles. "Hi Lizzie. I'm Amelia." She motioned over her shoulder. "That's Kirby."

Lizzie smiled. She stepped out of the caravan down two metal steps to the wet grass. "You *have* come about the boy, haven't you? The one who got snatched."

Kirby and Amelia shared a knowing look, and Kirby said, "That's right. He's lost and alone, and we want to bring him back home. Back to his mum and dad where he belongs."

Lizzie nodded.

"You live here, don't you?" added Amelia. "Seen anything unusual?"

The girl smiled. "I know secrets," she said.

"What kind of secrets?"

Lizzie didn't answer. Kirby was beginning to feel uneasy. Was it getting colder?

"Where are your parents, Lizzie?" Amelia asked. "Are they in the caravan?"

Lizzie ignored the question. "I'll tell you a secret. I'll show you what you want if you'll play a game with me."

"What sort of game?"

"Hide and seek," said Lizzie. "Come and find me, and I'll show you where the boy is."

Amelia reached into her yellow raincoat, pulled out her hazel wand, and the girl made a hissing sound. Her features changed, her face becoming a twisted sneer, her eyes turning black. But only for a moment, and then she was a girl again, smiling, playing with her hair.

A lump of fear crawled from Kirby's chest up into his throat. "It's her!" he said. "The witch!"

"Yes, thanks for that," said Amelia. "So glad you're here to dispense those nuggets of insight."

Kirby didn't have the chance to reply because the girl flickered at the edges, and grew and twisted until she was taller than the tallest adult Kirby had ever seen. Her legs were too long, her arms so elongated that her twisted fingers were almost touching the ground. Her face was still that of a young girl, but there were black circles around her dark eyes, and she had a mouthful of teeth sharp as needles.

In a single leap she was on top of one of the caravans, crouched down, her hair falling over her pale face. She began to sway from side to side, her hair swinging gently, and she sang, in the sweet voice of a child...

*Hide and go seek,*
*Hide and go seek,*
*Darkness is coming and shadows will creep.*

*A sweet child is lost.*
*Will he be found?*
*Or will he end up in a hole in the ground?*

She hissed at Kirby and Amelia, then she jumped down behind the caravan, disappearing from sight.

They sprinted around after her, but the only thing waiting was mist.

And then, her voice somehow so close to his ear that Kirby could feel her rotten breath, she said, "Come and find me."

"What do we do?" he asked. He was shivering, both with fear and with cold.

Amelia stared around the fairground. Everything was silent. Everything still. She looked back at Kirby. "We play."

"Play?"

"Just as she asked. We play hide and seek with her. If we find her, we'll find the missing boy. What's his name?"

"Charlie." Kirby paused. "This is probably a trap though, right?"

"Little tip for you, Kirby: any time the soul of an evil witch shows up and asks you to play hide and seek… pretty certain to be a trap."

"Right. And we're just going to walk into it?"

Amelia ran a hand through her wild hair.

"We have to find it first."

# The Haunted House

"So where do we start?" Kirby asked.

Amelia tapped her hazel wand against her forehead. "Right," she said, "let's think about this properly. She's taken on the form of a child."

"Aye, If you can call that thing a child." Kirby shivered at the thought of the witch's too-long arms and legs and fingers.

"Yes," said Amelia, "the point is she's childlike. So we're probably looking for something that would come from a child's mind... I don't know..." She turned away and began to wander through the mist. "A child. What would a child think of?"

"I hate to point out the obvious," Kirby said, enjoying the fact he might have thought of something before Amelia for a change, "but there are two children right here. I'm a child. So are you. Sort of. Aren't you?"

Amelia spun to face him, and marched through the rain-soaked mist towards him. "You're right!" she said. "You *are* a child! So what would you do, Kirby, if you had all of this to play with?" She motioned around the fairground. "Where would *you* set a trap?"

Kirby began to walk past stalls and rides, until something made him stop.

"Amelia?"

"Yes?"

"You see that haunted house there?"

"What, the one that looks like a real house? The one with the turrets? The one that fills me with a sense of dread?"

"That's the one. Well… it wasn't there yesterday."

"You sure?"

"Yeah. Me and Dad covered every inch of this place the other night. No haunted house. Plus, it's the perfect place for a trap, isn't it? Dark and spooky. Probably lots of places to hide."

Amelia gave him a smile. "You know what, Kirby Simpson? You're actually quite useful to have around. Sometimes." She nodded to the haunted house. "Shall we?"

The house looked very old. It was made mostly of stained black wood, with a wraparound porch like the houses from old movies, and a spire at one corner with a weathervane in the shape of a skull. The porch steps creaked and moaned as they climbed. When they reached the front door, its paint chipped and cracked, they stopped and listened.

Nothing.

Kirby was frightened, and he knew he was right to be frightened: whatever lay beyond the door was sure to be dangerous. But there was excitement in him too.

Amelia reached for the handle on the front door. It turned with a loud click, and she pushed it, letting it swing open. Then she stepped forward, into the house.

The door slammed shut in Kirby's face. "Amelia?" he said. "Open the door."

But Amelia did not answer.

Inside the haunted house, Amelia pulled on the door handle. It wouldn't budge. "Kirby!" she yelled. "Don't move!"

She rummaged in her yellow raincoat, pulled out her hazel wand, and held it up to the door. The end quivered ever so slightly. Amelia tapped on the door with the stick, but instead of the gentle click of wood against wood an enormous, deep clanging sound reverberated through the hallway. Amelia stowed the wand back in her raincoat.

"Kirby! Can you hear me?"

No answer.

"If you can hear me, stay exactly where you are. The door is sealed tight. It'd take me hours to open it. I'm going to go in alone. DO NOT TRY TO FIND A WAY IN WITHOUT ME, OK?"

Kirby still didn't answer.

"He's smart," Amelia told herself. "He won't do anything stupid. I hope."

Then she turned away from the door and crept further into the house.

Outside in the dark fog Kirby held his breath.

He waited.

Nothing happened. There was no sound from inside the house, no sign that Amelia was even still there.

He began to breathe normally again and tried the door, hoping it might open for him this time. It didn't. For a fraction of a second he considered going back to the wall by the main road, where a single policeman was keeping watch over the place. But what would he say?

"Excuse me, Officer, my friend (who's almost certainly a witch, by the way) and I broke in to the carnival tonight hoping to catch the soul of an evil witch who's risen from the dead. But now my friend (the witch, remember) has gone into a haunted house (one that wasn't here yesterday) and got trapped, probably by the ghost of the evil witch I mentioned a second ago..."

Somehow, he didn't think that story would go down well, and he didn't much fancy seeing Dad's face when he opened the door to see his son standing on the doorstep with a policeman in the middle of the night, accused of wasting police time.

"So," Kirby said to himself, "alone it is then."

Mist swirled around the haunted house as he creaked back down the porch steps to the wet grass. The rain was getting heavier, the wind picking up. Kirby pulled up the hood of his jacket and set off around the back on the hunt for another way in. It really was an impressive place; it looked like it had been there for a hundred years, like it had always stood in that field and the carnival had been put up around it.

Kirby did a full circuit, past the carousel on one

side of the house and around the back, where he half expected to find a garden. No garden, but there was a back door. It was locked. He raced back up the other side along a sort of alleyway between the house and a large striped tent where a magician performed. He checked every window only to find it locked. He stood in front of the house, arms folded in the lashing rain, and stared. He was just wondering if he could climb the porch when a voice to his right said, "Why don't you try the back door?"

Slowly, very slowly, Kirby turned his head. Through the mist he could see the carousel. And on it, sitting on a unicorn, was the witch. She was a little girl again, no longer stretched and warped, and Kirby was glad of that, he supposed. But knowing what she really was, that she could become a monster at any moment, made the blood in his veins chill.

"You shouldn't be frightened." The witch smiled an innocent smile, then a flash of wickedness crossed her face and she added, "Yet."

Kirby was aware, through the numbing fear, that his body was shaking. Any time he had encountered anything like this, Amelia had been at his side, protecting him, making him feel brave.

"I've already tried the back door," he said, sounding as calm as he could.

She smiled again and swung her legs over the back of the carousel unicorn, dropping to the ground, and walking with slow, deliberate steps towards Kirby, her long black hair falling over her face.

Kirby wanted to run, to turn and get away. But he couldn't leave Amelia. And he wouldn't give up on Mum. So he stayed perfectly still as she came closer and closer, until she was standing beside him, so close he could feel the icy air around her on his face.

She reached out, pulled down his hood and spoke, her lips so close they brushed his ear. They were cold as the winter sea. "Run, boy. Run to the back door. Your friend is suffering..."

Kirby launched himself forward, forcing his legs to move faster and faster, not looking back, because he knew she would be there, a step or two behind, toying with him.

When he reached the back door it creaked open, and he dashed into the dim room beyond. He stopped, and spun to see the door slam shut and the shutters on the windows all close with a snap, leaving him in darkness.

Behind him, somewhere in the haunted house, he heard the witch-girl laugh, and then she was silent, and he knew he was alone.

# The Shadow-Birds

Kirby's heartbeat thundered in his ears as he peered around the gloomy haunted house. He was standing in a long hallway lit by flickering gas lamps and lined with peeling, striped wallpaper.

"Amelia?" He edged along the passage. "Are you here?"

No answer.

Kirby tried the first door he came to, but it was shut tight. They all were.

"Amelia?" he called out, cringing at the boom of his voice in the silence. "Where are you?"

Still nothing. The only sound was the monotonous ticking from a grandfather clock. Everything smelled of dust and age, and something else, something sour, like spilled milk.

Kirby walked back towards the front door and turned to see a sweeping staircase that led to the first floor. He put one foot on the worn, stained carpet of the first step.

"You're getting warmer," said the voice of the witch in his ear. Kirby spun round, but the hallway was empty. A cold breath of air on his face gave him the shakes.

"Where are you, Amelia?" he said, and he slowly climbed the stairs.

As Kirby moved up the stairs, in another part of the house Amelia Pigeon fell to her knees, panting. She wiped a trickle of blood from her cheek and stowed her hazel wand back in her yellow raincoat. In front of her was a pile of mouldy, blood-stained bandages and dust. Up until a minute or so ago, the bandages and dust had been walking around in the form of a mummy with attitude.

A sound caught her attention, something twitching and scrabbling around. Amelia got back to her feet, straightened her raincoat, and spotted where the noise was coming from.

A hand wrapped in ancient bandages was inching across the floor, using its fingers as legs, trailing a ragged strip of material behind.

Amelia frowned. “Missed a bit.” She strode forward, raised a foot, and brought it down as hard as she could on the mummy’s severed hand. There was a cracking noise. One of the fingers stuck out from beneath the sole of Amelia’s boot, wriggling, scraping at the floor. She twisted her foot, and the finger, along with the rest of the hand, turned to dust.

“Very good,” said the witch-girl behind her.

“I could end this now.” Amelia turned to face her. “You know I could.”

“You could,” said the witch, “but you can’t destroy this spell without destroying the lost boy too.” She smiled a sweet, innocent smile. Then her teeth turned to needles. “Not to mention your little friend. He’s so brave, isn’t he?”

Amelia’s eyes widened. “Kirby? Kirby came in here?”

The witch laughed, and then was gone.

“You idiot, Kirby!” yelled Amelia. “I told you not to…” She ran for the door, which flew open, and she was out into the upstairs hallway. “Kirby!” she said. “Hold on. I’m coming!”

Somewhere else on the first floor, Kirby heard a distant door slam shut, the sound echoing around the house.

"Amelia? Is that you?"

He moved towards the sound, along a corridor lined with portraits of terrified-looking children. Some were crying, others screaming silently. Kirby stopped at a photo of a boy dressed in clothes from another age. His pale face peered out of the frame, his eyes hollow and sad. His thin hands were pressed, palms out, against the inside of the glass.

What happened next almost knocked Kirby from his feet. The boy in the photograph moved. With one fingernail he etched two words onto the inside of the glass.

HELP ME

Kirby closed his eyes and took a few slow, deep breaths. "You're not real," he said to the boy in the photograph. "You're an illusion. All of this is an illusion..."

The boy started to groan and pound the glass with his fists. Then the other portraits joined in, dozens of them on the walls, all moaning and punching and scratching. The noise grew and grew. Kirby clamped his hands to his ears, stumbled backwards, spun round and reached for the first door, turning the handle and darting into the room beyond.

He closed it behind him. The voices died away and Kirby slunk to his knees in the dark silence of a library.

Somewhere else on the first floor, Amelia Pigeon waved her hazel stick, and the creature that stood in her way, the one made from ten thousand beetles all stuck together, turned to ash and scattered.

"Now that's just rotten," said the witch-girl, suddenly at her side. "I liked that one."

Amelia spun, swiping at her, but her hand and the hazel passed right through the witch-girl.

"I'm not really here, silly," she said. "But you're getting closer."

"Where's Kirby? I swear, if you hurt him..."

"Who? Me? I wouldn't hurt him." She grinned. "But I can't say the same for some of the other stuff in here. Nasty."

"Call them off. Now. Or I'll—" Amelia stopped, because she was alone in the hallway again. "Hold on, Kirby, I'm coming."

The rows of bookshelves in the library were covered in thick dust. Cobwebs caught the light of the lamps like threads of shimmering silver.

Kirby walked between the rows of books touching the spines, running his hands along them, and found himself smiling. He imagined having a library like this for himself. Books had calmed and soothed him for as long as he could remember, and he found that he wasn't so worried about the witch any more.

Maybe the best thing to do was stay in one place and wait for Amelia to find him. He was sure she would, eventually. And what harm could come to him here, among books? Books were his friends. He reached up, took a small one bound in green leather from a shelf, and opened it. But the pages began to turn on their own, and Kirby dropped the book to the floor. The pages slowed, and were still.

It began as a gentle breeze. At first Kirby thought someone must have left a window open. Then he realised the library had no windows. The breeze brushed his face, his hair, and as it grew stronger a smell came with it, a smell like burning wood.

In the time it took to draw breath, a cloud of shadows exploded from the book Kirby had dropped, dozens and dozens of them. They flew to the high ceiling, fluttering in a flock. Each was the size of a bat – the same sort of black as the spiders. One of them broke from the group, blazing down towards Kirby. He ducked as it flew close overhead, calling out in a strange, echoing caw. Another followed, then several more, and Kirby saw that they were birds, with long sharp beaks and glossy feathers.

*Snap.*

"Ow, get off me!" A sharp pain pierced Kirby's head. He swung around, batted the bird away. Had it just pecked him?

*Snap.*

Another pain, another bird. He began to run.

Above, the cloud of shadow-birds called out, their caws echoing through the dark library, and they moved as one, flying low, swirling and flapping around Kirby.

*Snap, snap, snap.*

"Get away!" He turned another corner, sprinting along another passageway between shelves. They kept swooping, kept pecking, and every time they did Kirby became more frightened, more confused.

"Amelia!" he yelled. "Amelia! Help me!"

He wished he'd never come into the house.

*Snap.*

House… where was he anyway? He remembered bright lights… candyfloss…

*Snap. Snap, snap.*

He was here to do something important, to help Amelia find someone…

*Snap.*

This couldn't be real, could it? It must be a dream. Why would he be in an old house in the middle of the night?

*Snap.*

He'd better get home. Mum and Dad would be worried. Only… Mum… something had happened to Mum…

*Snap. Snap.*

Now he was unsure of anything. What was his name? Why did his head hurt so badly? Why was he running?

*Snap, snap, snap, snap…*

Kirby stopped, no longer frightened. He felt numb and didn't care what might happen to him.

The flock enveloped him. Everything went black. He could feel them, the wind from their wings, the sharp sting of their bills as they feasted on his memories and emotions. Soon there would be nothing left of him and he'd fall into a silent forever.

Everything stopped.

He opened his eyes.

The birds were all around him, but they were perfectly still. Frozen in the air. He brought a hand up, touched one of them. It was cold as ice.

"Kirby!"

There was a girl in a yellow raincoat standing a few paces away. Her hair was messy. She looked very worried.

"Hello," he said. "I don't know who Kirby is, but if I see him I'll tell him you're looking for him. What's your name?"

The girl in the yellow raincoat stared at him. Then she looked at the shadow-birds and a dark anger filled her eyes. "Give it back." Her voice seemed to amplify. "Everything you took from him."

"Quite pretty, aren't they, these birds?" said Kirby.

"No," said the girl in the yellow raincoat, "they are not." She looked up and around. "I mean it," she said. "Give his memories back. And anything else you took."

Somewhere in the library someone giggled. It sounded like a girl. "Spoil sport."

"Who was that?"

"Never mind."

It was as if Kirby's head had been an empty glass and someone had turned on a tap. It filled up with memories and emotions and knowledge.

He blinked. “What just happened to me?”

Amelia smiled, and sighed with relief. “Doesn’t matter now.” She reached up, touching one of the frozen birds with her finger. It turned to dust and fell to the floor. In a single burst, all the birds did the same, raining down with a soft hiss.

“What now?” said Kirby. He made a footprint in the bird-dust.

“Now?” Amelia answered. “Now we find the missing boy and finish this.”

# The Second Witch

They found him in the attic. A dark, narrow staircase led them to a door. Beyond the door, they brushed through curtains of cobwebs to find a large space filled with all manner of junk: from teetering towers of boxes to creepy mannequins, their faces illuminated by moonlight, which fell through the narrow windows in silver stripes. The place smelled strongly of damp, and of fear.

And there, sitting by the window at the far end of the attic, was the boy.

"Stick close," Amelia told Kirby as they edged closer. The boy had his back to them. He was in a small wooden child's chair, staring out of the window. "Charlie, is that you?"

The boy blinked. He turned his head and looked at them. He was only six years old, alone in a terrible place, but there was no fear in his eyes, just emptiness. He turned away, looking back to the window.

Amelia sat on the floor beside him, and Kirby followed her lead. Charlie did not look at them.

"We're here to help you," said Kirby. "To get you out of here. Take you home. Would you like that?"

"Home?" said the boy, and he looked at Kirby with a puzzled expression. "Home..." It seemed like he was trying to remember the word, what it meant.

Kirby took the little boy's hand. It was freezing cold and ghostly pale in the moonlight. When they touched, the boy looked into Kirby's eyes and his hand warmed up. Kirby could see that he was remembering.

"Home..." His brown eyes filled with tears. "I want home. I want Mummy and Daddy."

Kirby squeezed the little boy's hand tight. "We'll get you back to them." He looked to Amelia, who was standing up, glancing around.

"Kirby," she said, "I want you to get Charlie out of the house. Don't worry about me."

"What are you going to do?"

"I'm going to make sure she can't hurt anyone else." She turned towards Charlie and smiled. "Kirby is very brave. He's going to take you home. Stay with him, OK, Charlie?"

Charlie nodded, still holding Kirby's hand.

"She won't let us go," said Kirby. The room was growing very cold, and he shivered. "She'll try to stop us."

"No," Amelia reassured him. "She'll have enough to worry about. Now go."

Kirby pulled Charlie away, and they were off across the attic. As he reached the top of the stairs, Kirby stopped and looked back. Amelia was still standing by the window. Only now she wasn't alone.

"Come on," he said to Charlie. "Remember what Amelia told you. Stay with me."

"They'll never make it out, you know."

The witch-girl appeared from the shadows and stood in front of Amelia, smiling. "If you destroy my spell while they're still inside the house, you'll kill them. You know that." She put on a mock petted lip. "Oh my. We are in a tight spot, aren't we?"

"You have no idea how much trouble you're in," said Amelia. "You were better off in the graveyard asleep."

The girl hissed at her, and her tongue was black.

"Who brought you back?" said Amelia.

"Oh, I can't tell you that! It would spoil the surprise. Don't you like surprises?" The witch gave another wicked smile, which turned into a laugh, and then she spoke her spell, the old language ragged in the air.

Kirby was running through the house. He wanted to run faster, but Charlie was much smaller and his little legs couldn't keep up. The hallway on the first floor was different from before, longer. Lights on the walls flickered as if they'd been caught in a breeze. Then, one by one along the length of the passageway, the gas lamps blinked out until only one was lit, right beside Kirby and Charlie. The remaining lamp flickered and danced, but it did not go out. It kept the night at bay.

Charlie gripped Kirby's hand. "I'm scared of the dark, there's monsters in the dark. Mummy and Daddy got me a night light so I wouldn't be scared any more. It shines stars on my wall."

This made Kirby smile.

Then the last lamp went out.

Amelia picked herself up from the attic floor. She dusted off her yellow raincoat.

"They were wrong," said the witch-girl. "You're not so big and bad. You're old and weak. I can smell it."

"Who was wrong?" Amelia asked. "The people who woke you? Old I might be, but not weak..." She whispered a short burst of words, and a gale blew up, so strong that it knocked the witch backwards. She fought against it, wide-eyed, flailing.

As Amelia moved forwards, stalking the witch-girl, she thought of Kirby. He was in darkness, frightened. Something came to her then, a picture in her mind. Blue stars on a wall... a child's night light.

"Follow the stars," she said. "Follow them home, Kirby."

Charlie hugged Kirby tightly in the blackness. He was crying. Not screaming for show the way young children sometimes do. This was body-shaking, terrified crying.

A star appeared in the dark. It was blue and twinkling.

At first Kirby thought he was seeing things, but he felt Charlie shift in his arms, and the little boy turned around and saw it too. He said, “It’s my star. My night light. From home!” As he spoke another star appeared on the ceiling a little further along the hallway.

“It’s Amelia.” Kirby smiled. “It must be her. She’s showing us the way out!” He grabbed Charlie’s hand again. “C’mon,” he said. “Follow the stars, Charlie.”

# Follow the Stars

Outside, in a dark corner of the fairground, Brothers Swan and Swift stood in shadow, watching.

"This is nice," said Brother Swift, sweeping his greasy hair from his eyes. "Isn't this *nice*, Brother Swan? I haven't been to a carnival since..."

"Munich, when we made that Ferris wheel collapse." Brother Swan held a stick in his pale hand, and on the stick, where candyfloss might usually be, was a spider's web filled with dead flies. He took a bite, grinding the chewy flies between his teeth. "I can still hear the screams..."

Brother Swift smiled at the memory. He nodded at the haunted house. "You know, I think she's getting awfully close to the boy. She's fond of him."

Brother Swan wrinkled his long, crooked nose. "Disgusting," he said. "How she can be fond of any of them I'll never know. They're insects to be trampled, every single one."

"How about we make things a bit more interesting for her little friend, eh?" Brother Swift reached into his long coat, and when he pulled out his hand a spider, blacker than black, was nestling in his palm. He held the spider to his mouth, touching it to his lips, and whispered, "You're the last. They took away your family, all those brothers and sisters." He put the spider down on the wet grass. "Off you go, my beauty. Get your revenge."

The spider scurried away through the mist towards the house. As it moved it grew in bursts, and by the time it reached the haunted house its body was the size of a large rat, with legs as thick as a man's wrist.

When the spider had disappeared inside the house, Brothers Swan and Swift faded back into the misty darkness, and watched.

As Kirby and Charlie moved towards the stairs, the house began to shift and change. The wallpaper and the grain of the wood on the floor became more basic. The perspective bent and warped.

"What's happening?" said Charlie.

"I think Amelia's winning." Kirby didn't know this for sure, but it made sense to him; if this illusion of a house was fading, the witch's spell must be weakening.

They stood at the top of the staircase and stared down. Never before had climbing down a set of stairs been such a challenge. The stairs sat at different angles, twisted. One step seemed to be just a few inches high, the next a huge jump. Kirby had to climb down and drop from the edge of the last step, and then catch Charlie as he did the same.

The front door was only a few paces away now, and Kirby's heart filled with hope as they ran towards it.

A movement in the shadows above stopped them.

Something was lowering from the ceiling, something as big as a large rat, with eight long, thick legs. As it landed on the hallway carpet, blocking the way to the front door, Kirby felt a jolt of burning pain in his hand from the place the spider had burst through his skin. He knew beyond doubt that this was the same spider. His spider. Only everything about it had been magnified: the blackness of it, its fangs, its sparkling black eyes.

Charlie grabbed at Kirby's clothes as Kirby stepped forward. The spider reared back.

"Well... someone's been feeding you, haven't they?" said Kirby.

In a voice as dry as dead leaves, the spider spoke. "She's not here to protect you now, boy. We said we'd come for you. We keep our promises." Kirby reached into his coat and pulled out the hazel twig Amelia had given him.

"She's always with me," he said. "Always. Don't forget that."

The house rumbled and shook, throwing Kirby and Charlie to the ground. Kirby let go of the wand and saw it bouncing away across the hall. He stared after it, then at the spider.

The monstrous creature made a move, scurrying forward, coming at him with murderous intent. But Kirby grabbed Charlie and leapt, landing on his belly, skidding across the floor towards the twig. His fingers wrapped around it and he popped up, drawing a circle on the ground just as the spider was upon them.

It shrieked, leapt off him at once, and landed on the floor on its back a few metres away, twitching and writhing, its huge body sizzling and bubbling like melted cheese under the grill. After a few moments it was still as stone.

Kirby held the hazel out like it was a sword.

"C'mon," he said to Charlie, and they edged towards the door, the two of them, never turning their backs on the hallway, until they were out of the house, down the porch steps...

Free.

In the attic, Amelia stood over the witch, looking down on her with furious eyes. The witch-girl cowered and pawed at her face madly, her eyes wide with terror.

"You have a choice," Amelia told her. "I could bind you with this place, this carnival; trap you forever, always awake, always aware, always screaming to get out. I've done it before. Lots of times. There's another like you in the woodland not far from here. Only she took the form of a bear, not a child." She smiled. "That didn't work either."

"Do what you will," said the witch-girl. "It won't be as bad as facing them what brought me back."

Amelia stood very still. "No," she said, "what I do won't be as bad. It will be worse. Unless you help me."

The witch-girl spat on the floor, and her spit bubbled on the dry wood. "I can't," she said. "If they found out, they'd torture me forever.

There are worse things than death. Take it from someone who knows."

"Tell me who brought you back."

"No."

"If you do I'll take you back to the graveyard and let you rest. I know that's what you want. I know you don't want to do what they're telling you. I can feel it."

The witch slumped, sliding down the wall until she was crouching, like a frog. "I was fourteen when I died," she said. "Fourteen! They dragged me through the town, grown men and women, spitting at me. Calling me terrible things." She looked up pleadingly at Amelia. "I wasn't bad. I speak the old language but I didn't use it to hurt anyone. But they burned me anyway. You ever been burned?"

Amelia stared at her feet. She shook her head.

"You're right," said the witch. "I didn't want to come back. But I didn't have a choice. When those two showed up in the graveyard and woke me up I tried to fight them off. All I wanted was to stay asleep. But they were too strong. They dragged me out of the ground and said if I didn't do what they told me, they'd make sure I burned forever. I don't want to burn."

Amelia stared down at her. "There were two of them?"

"Aye."

"Describe them."

"Can't," said the witch-girl. "I'd only just woke up. I was confused."

"If you help me find who did this, I promise you won't ever have to worry about them again. You can rest deep. And I keep my promises."

The witch stared up, and she was the frightened child she'd been in life once more. "No burning?"

"No," said Amelia, "no burning."

The witch-girl nodded. "I can't tell you how they looked, but there was definitely two. I could smell the reek of them, the death and suffering they'd brought to the world." She stopped, and stared up at Amelia. "Your past smells a lot like theirs. There's pain there." Her eyes grew wide. "You've done bad things."

Amelia seemed to sway on the spot, like she was going to fall over, but she steadied herself and said, "What do they want? They must have let something slip. They must be here for a reason."

"Oh they are," said the witch. "They're here for the Shadowsmith. That's you, isn't it?"

Whatever she was thinking, Amelia's face was unreadable. She stared out of the attic window, and the silence was long and cold.

"Like I say, I keep my promises. I'll take you back to the graveyard."

The witch-girl looked up at her. "You can't beat 'em. You should run away, as far as you can go."

"The thing about running," said Amelia, "is if you do it hard enough, for long enough, you come back to where you started." She held out a hand. "Come on. Time for you to go back to sleep."

# Reunited

Outside, the mist and rain swirled around Kirby and Charlie.

"I want to go home," said Charlie.

"Just a minute or two more." Kirby stared at the front door of the haunted house, willing it to open, wishing Amelia would walk through it, down the porch steps, safe and whole and well.

"Can we go now?" said Charlie. "Please?"

"Charlie, just one minute more! The girl we left behind is my friend. I want to make sure she's alright."

"Friend?" Charlie screwed up his face. "You mean like a girlfriend? That's disgusting."

"No, Charlie. Not like a girlfriend..."

The creak of the front door interrupted them, and out walked Amelia. Her face was scratched and there was a bruise around her left eye, but she walked calmly, seemingly in no rush, along the porch and down the steps to the grass.

Kirby was so overjoyed to see her, so relieved she was safe, that he had to stop himself grabbing her and hugging her tight. He did not want to give Charlie any more fuel for the girlfriend fire.

"You showed us the way," he said. "You made stars shine on the ceiling."

"You saved yourself," Amelia replied. "Nice work."

"Are you his girlfriend?" asked Charlie.

Amelia looked down at him. "Most definitely not."

"What's that?" asked Kirby. Amelia was holding something, cradling it – a rag doll with long dark hair and white skin.

"It's a promise," she said, placing the doll gently in the pocket of her raincoat. "Come on. Let's get Charlie back to his mum and dad, eh?"

She stopped then, dead still, and her eyes grew wide as she sniffed at the air.

"Amelia?" Kirby waved a hand in front of her face. She didn't notice. Then she ran, full pelt, into the mist. "Amelia! Where..."

Kirby followed, dragging Charlie with him. They found Amelia a short distance away, on her hands and knees, scooping up globs of mud, rubbing them between her fingers, sniffing them.

"Um... Amelia?"

No answer. Amelia slipped one of her muddy fingers into her mouth and licked away the mud, swirling it around on her tongue.

"Amelia. Have you lost your mind?"

She stood up; she was shaking. "Home," she said. "Now."

"Are you going to tell me what's wrong?"

Amelia gave Kirby a stare so powerful it almost knocked him over. She was not joking.

So they hurried through the carnival, the three of them, back towards the town.

Charlie's house was a few lanes back from Kirby's, an old fisherman's cottage in the middle of a crooked row, with a bright blue door. There were no lights on; it was after two in the morning and Craghaven had fallen asleep to the tumbling lullaby of the North Sea.

When they reached the house Charlie made to knock on the door, but Amelia stopped him. "Just a minute longer," she said. She had calmed down a little, but she still seemed jumpy.

"I'm cold," said Charlie.

"I'm going to help you," Amelia told him. "What you've seen these past few days, where you've been… it'll stay with you, haunt you."

"I was brave," said Charlie.

Amelia reached out, touched his cheek. "You were ever so brave. But you see that's the trouble. Children *are* brave. Grown-ups are much more afraid of the world than children, Charlie."

The little boy screwed up his face. "Really?"

"Really?" Kirby echoed.

"Yup," said Amelia. "Memories of the witch and the haunted house and being away from home all alone – they'll all seem very different when you're an adult. You won't want to believe them, won't believe yourself. And if you don't believe yourself the world will eat you up. So I'm going to take those memories away."

For a moment there was only silence, and mist and rain.

"Will it hurt?" asked Charlie.

"No." Amelia stroked Charlie's hair. "It won't hurt."

She leaned over and began to whisper close to Charlie's face. Kirby watched her lips move, saw something drift out of the boy's ear, something like a coil of dark smoke. Amelia breathed it in and straightened up, holding her breath for a second or two. Then she let it out, and the dark smoke escaped her mouth, rising up into the mist, scattering to nothing.

"There," she said. "Now, you're going to knock on the door, and you're going to live a long, happy and normal life. Understood?"

Charlie nodded. He looked like he'd just woken up from a dream. He knocked on the door.

"Come on." Amelia pulled Kirby away, down the street a little, where they stopped to watch.

"Shouldn't we hide?" asked Kirby.

"Nah. They can't see us."

Squinting through the wet night, Kirby watched Charlie knock on the door more loudly. Seconds later the door opened and a woman stood in the doorway. When she saw little Charlie standing at the door, she stepped back and covered her mouth with her hands. Then she dropped to her knees and swept him up in her arms. "Oh Charlie!" she was saying. "My Charlie..."

As Kirby watched, he thought of his own mum, of her hugs. How he missed those hugs. Maybe, now they'd defeated two witches, she was waking up this very moment. He felt a warm glimmer of hope in his stomach.

Charlie's dad was at the door now, scooping Charlie up and kissing him, kissing his hair.

"You did that," Amelia told Kirby. Then, as Charlie's front door closed, she said, "We should go. We've one more job to do tonight."

# Back to Sleep

"We're back in the graveyard," said Kirby.

"Nothing gets past you, does it?" Amelia replied. "You really have honed your sense of observation into a finely tuned instrument."

"But *why* are we back? And how come you haven't conked out like you did last time you fought a witch?"

"I promised you, didn't I? We'll get you home first." Amelia had the rag doll in her hands. "Plus, this witch didn't fight as hard as the first one. The first witch *wanted* to wake up, *wanted* to inflict her anger on the world. But all this one wanted to do was sleep. You don't like getting up for school on a Monday morning, right? Well, imagine how much worse it'd be if you'd been asleep for four hundred years."

They had cut through the main part of the cemetery, past grand tombstones and paupers' graves to the overgrown patch of unconsecrated ground beyond the far gate. It was almost three in the morning, and the sky was lightening in the east. Behind them, the dark blade of the church spire rose up into the mist.

The three black candles were still in the ground. Amelia walked to the middle one, placed the doll on the long grass beside it, and stepped back. The candle burst into dazzling flame, piercing Kirby's eyes.

Then, standing before them, was the witch-girl from the haunted house.

Kirby fumbled backwards, almost tripping on overgrown weeds.

"It's fine," said Amelia. "She won't harm you. We're helping her."

"Helping?" said Kirby. "She kidnapped Charlie! She took my memories!"

"I gave them *back*," said the witch a little sheepishly. "All of them. You can check 'em if you want."

"That won't be necessary," Amelia said to the witch, then to Kirby, "She helped me. I promised to bring her back. She won't bother anyone else."

The witch-girl smiled and began to hum 'Rock-a-bye Baby' slowly, slightly off-key. "Before I go," she said, "a warning."

"Go on," said Amelia.

"The witch trials in my time were terrible. Lots of innocent people suffered. But sometimes they found someone who deserved what they got. Sometimes they got it right. Watch out for the last witch."

With this off her chest, the witch-girl smiled, and at once began to glow silver like the moon. Whispers of curling smoke drifted up from her feet, which were fading away. The fading crept upwards, like someone was pulling a loose thread, unravelling her piece by piece. When only her head and shoulders remained, floating in the air, something occurred to Kirby.

"Wait! Please wait! I have a question."

The witch-girl's head did not look amused by the interruption. "Make it quick, boy."

Kirby felt the question on his lips, burning. "What's it like," he said, "to die?" Amelia gave him a pitying look, and he blinked the wetness from his eyes. "Does it hurt?"

"Well, I was burned in a bonfire..." said the witch-girl, "so what do *you* think? I remember a flash of pain, but after that... darkness wrapped around me like a blanket and lifted me away and I slept deeply, and I was happy."

"But..." Kirby was grasping around, trying to find the words, "can you still see what's going on in our world? Can you see living people? Can you hear us?"

The witch-girl opened her mouth to answer, but before she could speak the last of her unravelled, and she was nothing but smoke, drifting forever.

Kirby felt Amelia's hand in his, gripping tightly. "Come on," she said. "Let's get you home."

The walk back was quiet. Neither of them spoke, and the only sounds were their footsteps on the winding streets and the whisper of the rain. Amelia was walking slower than usual. Kirby knew she was tired, knew she needed to sleep, and by the time they reached his front door on Harbour Street she was pale as the witch-girl's ghost.

"You best go in," she said. "Your dad won't have a clue you've been gone this time. I've made sure of it."

"When will you come back?"

"When I'm ready. Go see your mum. Take her hand. Feel how warm it is. Alive. It'll help."

Kirby nodded. "When we were in the haunted house," he said, "the spider came back."

"What? Are you alright? Did it hurt you?"

"I'm fine, honestly. I used the hazel wand. I think I killed it."

"You think?"

"Well, there wasn't much time, was there? The place was falling apart. Last I saw the spider was on its back sizzling. Looked pretty dead to me."

Amelia drummed the tips of her fingers together. "Right. Good. Just be careful. Keep your hazel with you." She stopped and looked up. Then she pulled out her wand, pointed it upwards, and something fell from the gutter above, landing at their feet on the pavement with a slap. The thing was the size of Kirby's forearm, with loads of legs and a fat, pulsating body. One end of it rose up towards Kirby and opened up, forming a circular hole filled with sharp teeth. It hissed.

Amelia brought her foot down hard on the thing, and it exploded under her Wellington, leaving a puddle of dark pus and twitching legs on the ground.

"What a lovely way to end the night," said Kirby, fighting the urge to be sick. He opened the front door and stepped inside. The warmth of his house, and the smell of it, reminded him of Mum. "See you soon?"

Amelia nodded. "Get some rest." She flicked her hand and the door swung shut.

Inside, Kirby stood on his toes and stared through the peephole.

The street was empty. He turned, leaned against the door and looked around the hallway. It was good to be home.

# A Dark Dream

Brothers Swan and Swift stood over Kirby's bed, watching his chest rise and fall as he slept. They were taller than tall, their clothes darker than the darkest shadow.

"What do we do with him?" Brother Swan picked his large crooked nose and flicked black snot onto Kirby's bedroom floor. "We could give him a dose of the plague. Or drive him mad with nightmares?"

Brother Swift held up a hand, his eyes darting around. "Or," he said, "we could make him useful."

"How do you mean?"

"I mean, we could use him to our advantage. The thing about Little Miss High-and-Mighty these days is, she has a weakness. She cares about these people. Cares about *him*. So we use him to get at *her*."

Brother Swan swept a hand across his bald head.

He smiled, showing a row of pointed teeth. "I like it. Mother will be so proud."

Brother Swift gave a nod. He raised a long, white finger, leaned over the bed, and reached out, touching his fingertip to Kirby's forehead. He pressed gently, keeping contact for a few seconds, and then he let go and straightened up.

In the bed, the boy wriggled under his covers and kicked out a leg restlessly.

"There," said Brother Swift, "the seed's been planted. Now we let it grow."

And with that, Brothers Swan and Swift vanished into the early-morning gloom.

Kirby dreamed of Ruby Island, just off the coast. He was in a boat, the same rowing boat Amelia had used to reach the sea cave when they went to fight the spiders. But this time he was alone, rowing against the tide, being tossed around by the swell of huge waves.

He rowed and rowed, not knowing why, only knowing that he had to reach the island, that it was a matter of great importance.

Craghaven grew more distant, and the island loomed. When he was almost there, his arms throbbing and his shoulders ready to drop off, he looked at the water and saw that it had turned red. Turned to blood.

Fear stuck in his throat, choked him, but he rowed on – his little boat leaving a wake in the sea of blood – until he felt sand under him, and he came to a stop on a small beach among the rocks. He hopped out of the boat and ran up the beach to a staircase cut into the cliff. The steps zigzagged this way and that, up the cliff face, and when he reached the top his breath burned in his lungs.

The lighthouse was up ahead, and beyond that the flat expanse of the little island, sloping down in a wedge shape towards the sea at the far end. Halfway across he could see the standing stones jutting up out of the ground, and people standing around them. One was wearing a yellow raincoat.

As he ran forward, a flash of light engulfed the stones and he was knocked backwards by the force of it. When he landed, Kirby sat up, panting, sweating. He was on his bedroom floor, a tangle of covers wrapped around him.

Picking himself up, he moved to his window, opened the curtains, slid up the sash, and breathed in the still sea air. Something caught his eye through the mist. Out beyond the harbour there was a faint light in the water. He strained to see and thought, for a moment, that he glimpsed a rowing boat heading out to the open water – to Ruby Island. He blinked, and when he looked for the boat again, the mist had swirled around it and it was gone.

# FOUR

# The Island

# Fishing

When Kirby opened his curtains the next morning, he was amazed to see clear blue sky and sunshine. He threw the window wide, breathing warm summer air, and dressed in a hurry. Dad was already up, frying bacon and eggs. "Breakfast?"

"Please. I'm starving!"

The bacon was delicious; if there was one thing Dad could cook well, it was a fry-up.

"Seeing as the weather's taken a turn for the better, how about I take you out on a wee fishing trip?"

Kirby gulped down a mouthful of bacon. "Today?"

"Aye," said Dad. "Why not? Pete's done the lobster fishing for the day. Sea's calm. We'll take the fishing rods and a wee picnic. Come on." His eyes were pleading, and Kirby realised that he was asking for help, asking for an escape for a few hours.

"Sounds good," he said.

Kirby had fished before – living by the sea you couldn't really avoid it – but it had always been harbour fishing, casting off from Craghaven shore. Sometimes he'd drop a crab-line in near the edge with mussels and whelks as bait, and when he'd pull the line up there might be a crab or two on the end.

Fishing from a boat was quite different. For a start, Kirby was about as comfortable on the open water as a lobster on a bicycle. Even though the sea was calm, the boat still moved up and down with the soft waves, and it was hard to keep his balance. The first spot they tried they didn't catch a thing, so Dad moved them further out, and Kirby watched Craghaven grow smaller and smaller as the boat moved into the deep blue.

When they passed Ruby Island a sense of unease crept over Kirby. Flashes of his dream came back to him: the sea turning to blood, the figures by the standing stones. He stared up at the cliffs, at the thousands and thousands of seabirds, and he wondered if the dream meant anything. He remembered a time before he met Amelia when dreams were just dreams and didn't need thinking about twice.

Dad stopped the boat and they cast their lines in again, letting the weight take the bait down deep. Then he opened the cool box and brought out big, chunky sandwiches made with crusty bread, thickly spread butter and roast beef.

"So," he said, sitting back, the boat rocking gently, "I've been speaking to Frankie in the café. Says he's seen you with a girl." He smiled, and Kirby felt his face grow red. "What's her name?"

"Amelia."

A pause.

"Well?" Dad prodded. "Tell me more! Where's she from? What age is she?"

Kirby thought very carefully about his answer.

"She looks around my age," he said. "She's not from round here."

"On holiday with her family?"

"Something like that, yeah."

Another pause. The sea lapped against the side of the boat. It sounded playful, like it was chuckling.

"She's not my girlfriend, you know."

"Whatever you say, pal."

"But she's really not!"

"Fish," said Dad.

"What?" said Kirby.

"Look at your line. You've a fish on!"

Kirby stared at his fishing rod; it was quivering so gently he almost missed it, and there was the slightest bend near the tip. He leapt up, grabbed the rod.

"I've got a fish! I've got a fish! What do I do?"

"That's it," said Dad. "Pull the rod up for a few seconds, then point the tip back down at the water and reel. Good. Again."

After five minutes, Dad leaned over the side and grabbed the line, pulling it in, and Kirby finally saw what he'd caught. It was a large flatfish, dark brown in colour with a white underside.

"Well done, son!" said Dad. "Here, you hold it. I want a picture of this..."

The fish was heavier than it looked, slippery and cold. It didn't struggle as Kirby held it. He was as gentle as he could be while Dad took photos on his phone. Kirby hadn't seen him this happy since before Mum's accident, and all because Kirby had agreed to come out on the boat. It seemed like such a small thing, but to Dad it was obviously a big deal, and Kirby was glad to have made him happy. In some ways, Dad was just as much of a kid as Kirby.

"Why so many pictures?" Kirby asked.

"Are you kidding? Mum will be so gutted to have missed this. I'm covering every angle so she can see properly when she wakes up." He took a few more pictures. "Come on," he said with a huge grin, "let's put him back."

# Life or Death

"I do find these places infuriating," said Brother Swift.

"What? Hospitals?" said Brother Swan. "I don't think they're infuriating. Moreish? Yes. Morbid? Absolutely, in the best way. Infuriating? Never. There's too much lovely suffering to enjoy. Relax brother, and soak up the pain and misery."

"But it's these little people, isn't it?" said Brother Swift. "They think they know about the world. Think their medicine and their science has cracked it. Pah! They don't know anything. They never will."

The brothers were standing in a private room. Kirby's mum was lying in a hospital bed, hooked up to a ventilator and many other machines. Kirby sat at one side, reading aloud from a book. His dad sat at the other, holding his wife's hand. They were not aware of the brothers' presence.

"Oh, let's just kill her and be done with it."

The bright lights of the hospital gleamed on Brother Swan's bald head.

"If we do that," said a thoughtful Brother Swift, "the boy might give up altogether. We need him to be useful if the plan is going to work. We're nearly there. The third witch is waiting, and my word isn't she a treat. We just need to spur the child into action."

Brother Swan huffed. "On the other hand, if the boy's mother dies," he reasoned, "he'll be angry. Probably hell-bent on revenge. Careless. He might be more useful that way, hmm?"

Brother Swift wrapped a greasy strand of black hair around his finger, as he always did when he was deep in thought. "We'll flip a coin," he said. "Heads, the boy's mother dies. Tails, we just give him a good fright. Agreed?"

"Agreed."

Brother Swan reached into his coat and pulled out a coin that had been ancient even when the Vikings were raiding towns along the coast. He flipped it into the air and caught it, his bony fist closing over it. Slowly he opened his hand, and the brothers gazed down at the winning side of the coin.

"Well then," said Brother Swan, "that decides it."

Kirby was halfway through a chapter when the alarm sounded on one of the machines in Mum's room. It was a harsh, buzzing sound, and it made him jump. Dad leapt to his feet, and in what seemed to Kirby like one second the room was filled with people.

There were nurses and doctors crowding around, their hands busy, checking screens, shining torches into Mum's eyes. And among the sea of bodies, Kirby and Dad were being shepherded out into the corridor.

"What's happening?" Dad was yelling. "What's happening to her?"

The hospital people could only be heard saying, again and again, "We're finding that out now, Mr Simpson. It's best if you and your son step back and let us do our job..."

And then Kirby and Dad were in the corridor, the curtains in Mum's room were drawn, and they were hugging each other, crying, feeling lost and helpless and confused.

*Knock, knock.*

Kirby was lying on his bed, staring at the ceiling.

*Knock, knock.*

"It's me," Dad called from out in the hall. "You awake? Can I come in?"

"Aye."

The door creaked open, and Dad came in and sat on the edge of the bed. He stared at his hands for a moment, as if he was trying to find the right words. At last he said, "I'm just off the phone with the hospital. They said there was some sort of malfunction with one of the machines. Said they've never seen it before. She's still stable. She was lucky."

Kirby scoffed. "She didn't look lucky."

"She's still here," said Dad. "You OK?"

"Yeah. Just got a fright."

"Me too." He leaned over and ruffled Kirby's hair. "Try to get some sleep, eh?"

Kirby nodded, watched his dad leave the room. Then he got up and went to the window, sliding it open, letting the night air stream in. The mist was rolling in again, thick and damp, and the wind was picking up.

Out in the bay, the lighthouse on Ruby Island was flashing, its light cutting through the mist every few seconds like a blade.

*Everything changes so quickly*, Kirby thought.

In just a single flash of the lighthouse beam, he could have lost Mum. But she was still clinging on.

Still fighting. Life these past few weeks had been like that – changing in a flash, bringing the unexpected; bringing storms and witches and Amelia Pigeon.

And it wasn't done yet.

# The Second Storm

"Kirby! Wake up!"

"Hmm?"

"Wake up! C'mon!"

"Amelia?"

"No, it's not Amelia. It's Dad. Wake up!"

The world was a fuzzy tangle of confusion. Kirby sat up, rubbed his eyes. "Dad? What's that noise?"

"It's the wind." Dad was at the window, opening the curtains. Rain battered against the glass. The wind howled and moaned through the narrow street.

Kirby was awake now, his mind clearer. Dad was in his waterproofs.

"Why are you wearing that?"

"Because there's been a distress signal from a ship somewhere out near the bay. We're the nearest lifeboat station."

"You're going out? In that?"

"That's the idea."

Kirby stared out at the hammering wind and rain. Down the street Kirby could see the spray from massive waves crashing over the harbour wall.

"Mrs Coppershot next door will look after you while I'm gone," Dad said.

"But..." Kirby's body was flooding with panic, "you can't go!"

"I have to."

"No you don't! You're a volunteer! You can say no!"

"And why would I do that? People are in trouble."

"Because I don't want you to leave me! Everyone is leaving me!"

The words hung in the air, almost visible. Dad tilted his head a bit, staring at Kirby, his mouth open. He pulled him into a huge hug, his hands in Kirby's hair.

"You listen to me," he said. "Nobody is leaving you. Mum hasn't left you. She's fighting as hard as she can to come back to us. And it'll take more than a wee storm to separate me from my boy. I promise."

They sat on the edge of the bed. Kirby wiped his eyes.

"I have to help, son. Imagine it was me out there, stuck, in danger. You'd want someone to help me, wouldn't you? These people have families. Maybe even children that go to your school."

Kirby closed his eyes for a moment.

"I know. You have to go." He hated saying the words, but he knew they were right. He also knew this was no ordinary storm. The last witch was making a move, he was certain of it. "Just be careful," he said. "Please Dad. There's something weird about this storm, I can feel it."

"I'll say!" Dad laughed. "It's July. Must be global warming."

"No, I don't mean that. I mean... just please be careful. Extra careful. Promise?"

"Aye," said Dad. "Promise."

Somehow, this didn't make Kirby feel any better.

# A Nice Cup of Tea

Mrs Coppershot lived right next door, at number nine in the row of old terraced fisherman's cottages. She had been there forever, it seemed. Kirby quite liked her. She was really old and a bit deaf, but she always gave him a present at Christmas, and he'd sometimes take her dog Mylo out for a walk because Mrs Coppershot didn't get out as much as she used to.

Dad had been gone for over two hours, and the storm wasn't waning at all. If anything, it had grown stronger. Kirby and Mrs Coppershot were sitting at the front-room window watching the waves thundering against the harbour wall, the foam and spray whipping up in great peaks of white, when the doorbell rang.

Nobody had come up the street from the harbour. Neither had they come down the hill from the rest of town. Kirby stared at Mrs Coppershot. She stared back at him, the deep wrinkles in her face arranged in a picture of confusion.

"Who the devil is out in this?" she said. "They'll get themselves killed!"

She went to the door as fast as she could manage, which was not very fast at all. Kirby followed behind, hoping beyond hope that it was Dad, that somehow they just hadn't noticed him walking up the road, that he was back, safe and well.

But when Mrs Coppershot opened the door, it was not Dad who stood before them.

There were two men, dressed all in black. Both were very tall and very thin. One had long, greasy hair and the other was completely bald. They looked down at Kirby and Mrs Coppershot and smiled. Their smiles made Kirby feel uneasy.

One of the men, the one with the hair, said, "Hello, dear. You're going to invite us in for a nice cup of tea, aren't you?"

Kirby stared at Mrs Coppershot. Her face had gone strangely blank.

"Yes..." she said in an absent-minded sort of way. "Yes I am. Come on in out of the rain."

The men stepped into the hallway, brushing past Kirby, and he caught the scent of damp and rot coming from them. Mrs Coppershot closed her front door and followed them into the living room, Kirby at her heels.

"Who are they?" he whispered.

"Oh... I'm not sure," she said in that strangely vacant manner. "But they're nice, aren't they?"

"No," said Kirby. "No, Mrs Coppershot, they aren't nice."

But she didn't seem to hear him.

The living room was warm and cosy, filled with the many trinkets and ornaments Mrs Coppershot had picked up on travels with her husband a lifetime ago. The two men in black sat on the couch, while she toddled into the kitchen to make some tea. Soon they were sat, the four of them, listening to the crackle of the open fire as the gale roared outside.

Kirby shifted in his seat. Something about these two was familiar... and something was very off. He wished Amelia would knock on the door, sweep into the house and sort everything out.

The bald man sipped his tea, his face wrinkled in disgust. "This tea is horrific." He reached out and poured the contents of the cup onto the carpet.

Mrs Coppershot smiled at him as if he'd just told her she made the most delicious tea in all the world.

"You can't do that!" said Kirby.

"I think you'll find we can do what we like, sonny Jim," said the bald man.

"What do you want?"

The other man, the one with straggly black hair, stared at Kirby with close-set eyes that sparkled like black jewels in the light of the fire. "We're here to give you a warning, Kirby Simpson."

"Oh," said Mrs Coppershot, "that's *nice*."

Kirby realised what felt so familiar about these two. It was something in the air around them, a crackling static that he'd only ever felt once before.

"Has something happened to Amelia?"

"You want to watch that one, sunshine," said the bald-headed man. "She's tricky."

"Just tell me," said Kirby. "Is she in trouble?"

"Not yet," said the long-haired man, "but she will be. There's a witch over on the little island out in the bay. We reckon it's this witch who's making the weather go all haywire. Your friend is heading out there now. But this witch is so strong..." He gave a sad shake of his head. "Your friend doesn't know what she's in for."

"She's going there?" said Kirby. "Now?"

"Oh!" The long-haired man looked shocked. "She didn't tell you? Oops."

"No, she didn't." Kirby sat back in his chair and looked around the room, from the vacant smile of Mrs Coppershot to the faces of the two strangers. He wasn't stupid. He knew they were up to something. But if Amelia really was in trouble and he did nothing about it, he'd never forgive himself. "You're like her, aren't you?"

The men looked at each other. "You could say that."

"So you can help her?"

Their eyes widened in mock surprise. The one with the hair pressed a thin, bony hand to his chest. "Oh, no," he said. "We don't get involved in matters such as this. We wouldn't normally have come here to talk to you... only..." Something hung in the air, something he was holding back.

"Only what?"

"Only... your dad. He's out in the storm, isn't he?"

Kirby gripped the arms of the chair. "That's right. On the lifeboat."

"Oh dear," said the man. "Oh deary dear. We thought so, didn't we, Brother Swan? See, this witch is getting stronger. This storm is only going to get worse. And if it does... well, I don't fancy your dad's chances out there on the sea."

Kirby stood up, panic swirling in his head,

making him dizzy. The dream came back to him, the one with the sea of blood and the explosion by the standing stones on Ruby Island. "I need to go."

Mrs Coppershot looked up from her tea. "Have a lovely time, Kirby dear."

Kirby raced to the front door and threw on his raincoat. He had one hand on the door handle when he realised he was about to leave poor Mrs Coppershot alone with the two strange men. Rushing back to the living room, he said, "I think you should leave now..."

But the couch was empty. Mrs Coppershot was asleep, barking out snores from the comfort of her armchair.

The only signs the two men had ever been there were a pair of cups on the table, one empty, the other full, and a tea-stain on the carpet.

Kirby covered Mrs Coppershot with a knitted blanket, put out the fire, and rushed out the door into the raging storm.

Outside in the street, Brothers Swan and Swift stood in the driving rain and watched the boy coming out of the old woman's house. He hurried to the next door along and stumbled inside, reappearing a minute later only to dash away down the street towards the harbour. He ran right past the brothers without seeing them.

"Well," said Brother Swift, "I think that went well, don't you?"

"Very well indeed," said Brother Swan. "Shall we?"

And they walked, in no great rush, down the winding road after Kirby. As they went, the wild rain whipped around them, but they did not get wet.

# A Dangerous Journey

Kirby shut Mrs Coppershot's front door, then turned and fought his way up the street towards his own house, the screaming wind and rain pushing him back every step of the way. At his own front door, he fumbled in his pockets for the keys and, half blinded by the rain, managed to push it open.

The keys to Dad's lobster boat were hanging on their hook in the kitchen as always. He took them down, stuffed them in his raincoat and ran to the door, darting out into the storm once again. Then it was down the hill, past the cosy glow of Mrs Coppershot's window to the harbour.

The tide was high, the water black and churning. The boats anchored in the harbour seemed huddled together as if frightened by the angry sea. Some of the scaffold the harbour repairmen had been using was broken and twisted, and another section of the wall had crumbled. Dad's boat was halfway along. Kirby climbed down the slippery metal ladders, clinging on as he was battered by great gusts, and jumped onto the deck. The cabin offered some shelter.

"This can't be happening," he said to himself as his fingers probed his coat pocket for the keys. He'd watched Dad doing this hundreds of times. "Right... where's the ignition?"

*Aha!* Kirby found the slot, inserted the key and turned. The boat coughed to life; it vibrated and juddered beneath his feet, but the sound of the old engine was lost to the storm. He hurried out to the deck, unhooking the rope from the harbour to free the boat, which began to bob and drift. He grabbed a lifejacket and slipped it on. Then he was back inside the cabin at the wheel.

*What am I doing?* he thought. *This is the craziest thing anyone's ever done. Now what? How do I make it go?*

Before he could attempt to do anything else, the engine revved, sending a billow of smoke into the night. The boat shot forward, the wheel turning as if steered by an invisible helmsman as it moved out through the harbour.

Frightened and confused, Kirby grabbed the wheel and tried to turn it – to gain control – but it wouldn't budge.

Something made him look back then, towards the harbour wall, and he saw the two men from Mrs Coppershot's house, tall and thin and dressed all in black, watching him. One of them gave him a little wave. Kirby did not wave back. He turned again, looking through the windscreen just as the boat made a sharp turn out to the open sea.

No longer protected by the harbour walls, the boat was tossed around in the huge, foam-peaked waves. Kirby tried to wedge himself into a corner, tried to hold on to the seat and the railings in the cabin, but his grip failed and he staggered and rolled around as the boat moved up and down… up and down… in a sickening rhythm. Save for the faint twinkle of lights from Craghaven, all Kirby could see was darkness and mist as he tried desperately not to think of the deep, dark water beneath him. The occasional flash of lightning gave glimpses of what lay further out to sea: enormous, churning waves waiting to swallow him up.

Onwards the boat charged, climbing great mountains of water, splashing down, the bow stabbing through the surface. At the peak of every wave, Kirby caught sight of Ruby Island Lighthouse, its light carving through the darkness – one flash, then two, then three…

And with every wave, every flash of light, he was moving closer to the island.

A thought struck him. Maybe Amelia was the one controlling the boat. Maybe she was bringing him to the island. Maybe she'd be waiting for him with one of her smiles.

The thought made him braver, stronger, more determined, and the storm intensified around him, roaring as if it knew he wasn't afraid any more and it wanted to break him.

The boat curved a path around the back of Ruby Island, until at last it approached a small jetty sheltered between high cliffs. The waves died away and Kirby was able to come out of the cabin and look properly around. The fog was cotton-wool thick out here. Kirby could almost feel it pressing against him. Huge craggy cliffs rose from the mist behind the jetty, looming over him and his boat, and atop them was the lighthouse.

Dad's boat came to a stop. Kirby tied it to the jetty and climbed out. A short walk, huddled against the wind and rain, and he reached a set of steps hewn from the cliff face winding up and away towards higher ground.

"Kirby?"

The voice was almost lost in the gale, but he heard it and turned to see her, wearing her yellow raincoat as always.

"Amelia!"

Kirby ran towards his friend and wrapped his arms around her, hugging her tight. But she didn't hug back. He let go, took a step back. Her face was fierce.

"You, boy, are daft! Soft in the head! What are you doing here?"

"They said you were in trouble."

"Who did?"

"The men who came to see me."

"What men?"

"There were two of them," said Kirby. "One bald and one with long dark hair. They knew all about you. They told me you were in trouble."

"Do I look in trouble to you?" Amelia brushed soaking hair from her eyes.

"They told me there's a witch here on the island, and if we don't stop her my dad'll die. I'm frightened, Amelia. He went out in the storm on the lifeboat."

The anger faded a little from her face. She peered over his shoulder, back towards the jetty. "You stole your dad's boat?"

"Borrowed."

“You can’t drive a boat.”

“I didn’t have to.” He explained how it had brought him here seemingly by magic. “I thought it might have been you.”

“Not me.”

“Then who? The weird guys in black?”

Amelia looked troubled. Kirby could see her working things out in her head. Then she looked around as if checking whether anyone was watching. For the first time she seemed spooked.

“We need to move. Come on.” She grabbed his hand and led him to the steps in the rocks, and they began to climb.

# Brave

Nobody lived on the island these days. Engineers from the mainland regularly serviced the lighthouse, and sometimes expeditions of birdwatchers would visit to observe the many species of seabirds that nested in the cliffs. Apart from that, nobody set foot on the place.

Amelia opened the lighthouse door with no great trouble and soon they were inside, sitting on the spiral steps, the whole place banging and creaking in the wind. The interior was bare and grey, all chipped paint and plaster. A rusted metal banister curved up and out of sight, and a cold breeze breathed down the concrete steps from above.

"I can't believe you came here without me," said Kirby. "Really. After all the times I've helped you. You said I'd done well!"

"I know what I said." She folded her arms.

"You know why I didn't bring you? To protect you! That's out the window now, isn't it? Eh?"

"I wouldn't have come at all if those two weirdos hadn't shown up. They confused me. They got in my head."

"It's what they do," said Amelia. "I should never have let you get involved. Stupid. They know they can use you to get to me."

"Who?" said Kirby. "Enough with the mystery, Amelia. Please! I'm here now, there's nothing I can do about that. Look, I've already almost lost my mum because of this witch. I'm not going to watch her take my dad."

Amelia shook her head, muttering under her breath. "Those men who paid you a visit, I've known them for a long time."

Kirby raised an eyebrow. "*How* long a time are we talking?"

"Long," said Amelia. "Look, imagine the most evil, dangerous thing you can. Well, whatever that might be, it's about as threatening as a litter of puppies compared to these two. I've been putting the pieces together for a while now. I could feel something in the background as soon as I got here, something making it difficult for me to see clearly, to make sense of things. It was them – Swan and Swift."

Kirby sniggered. He couldn't help it. "Swan and Swift? Really?"

Amelia gave him a scornful look. "There's nothing funny about them. They'd slit your throat as soon as look at you – if you're lucky. They're the ones who brought the witches back. They're behind all of it. I can see it now."

"Why?" asked Kirby. "What could they possibly want in a little place like Craghaven?"

Amelia's green eyes were almost glowing in the darkness of the old lighthouse. "Me," she said. "They need me. They need my help with something, and it's not good."

"And you'd never help them, right?"

"Not by choice."

"And they know that?"

"Oh, they know."

"Are they stronger than you?"

A pause.

"There are different kinds of strength, Kirby."

Kirby found his mind wandering to the night Amelia had first turned up in his life. "When we first met you asked me if I was brave. Remember?"

She nodded.

"And I didn't know the answer. I didn't know what to say. But I do now. I know I can be brave.

But I also know that to be brave you have to be frightened first, and do your best to beat it. You taught me that. And you're the bravest person I've ever met."

Amelia looked at him, and smiled. "That means a lot, Kirby Simpson, coming from you."

"We can do this," said Kirby. "We can beat them."

Amelia was on her feet. "It has to be me. Understand? They're too strong. You'll do nothing. You will stay by my side and keep quiet, and maybe, if you're really lucky, you'll make it out of this with all your limbs."

Kirby nodded. "You've got a plan?"

"I'm going to clean up the last of their mess," she said. "Get rid of the last witch. Stop this storm."

"Then?" asked Kirby.

She took his hand, and led him to the front door, and the darkness, and the storm.

"Then?" she said. "Then, Kirby... I honestly don't know."

# The Last Witch

Walking the cliff tops was dangerous in such weather. The mossy grass was bumpy and littered with rocks, and although they kept well back from the edge, Kirby knew it would only take a stumble or slip and he'd be falling to the rocks and freezing water far below. The waves thundered against the cliff face, and the wind and rain drove at them without mercy.

The further Kirby and Amelia walked along the jagged coastline, the more the island tapered down towards the sea, until Kirby was no longer afraid to look over the edge.

Amelia tapped him on the arm. "Here," she yelled over the din. She pointed into the mist, where dark shapes gathered... buildings. As they moved closer Kirby could see that they were ruins, the skeletal remains of stone cottages, abandoned many years ago. There were six of them, all in a row – one nothing more than a lopsided wall, others more complete.

The third witch stood in the doorway of the last ruin.

She was not a bear, like the first.

She was not a child, like the second.

She was made of rain.

She was an ever-shifting mass of water, roughly the shape of a woman. Sometimes, when the wind caught her, it sent ripples across her surface, destroying her features, but a moment later they would reform. The rain was always adding to her, and every part of her, from her fingers to the shape of her hair, was always giving water back to the storm. When lightning lit up the world, it reflected on her body, made her dazzlingly bright.

She spoke, and her voice was the wail of the wind. "You've come to stop me?"

Amelia stepped in front of Kirby. "Go," she told him. "Hide." She pushed him away, and he half ran, half stumbled towards the nearest ruin, where he hid behind a wall, peering back through the rain. The witch seemed to have no interest in him; her gaze was fixed on Amelia, her watery locks of hair flicking around her head in waves.

"Stop the storm," said Amelia. "Now."

The witch laughed, and her laughter became a rumble of thunder. Overhead, the clouds swirled and churned, and beyond the island the sea was wilder than ever.

"I *am* the storm," she said. "The storm *is* me. And we're too strong for you now, girl." She shouted something in that strange old language, but when it came from the witch it was like a roar of the sea, crushing and violent.

She whipped her hands around and sent a ball of water tearing towards Amelia, who didn't react in time; it struck her in the face, sent her flying backwards, and she landed with a sickening crack on a jagged rock.

Amelia lay still for what seemed to be an age. Kirby watched her, his eyes wide, pleading, "Get up. Get up, Amelia."

She stirred.

Back on her feet now, she swept hair from her eyes. Blood streamed down her face from a deep cut on her hairline where she'd bashed her head on the rocks. "You won't win."

"I disagree."

"Do you know how many of your kind I've seen off in my time?" Amelia's voice was growing in power. "Too many to count."

"None like me," said the storm-witch. "Do you know how long I have waited for this? I warned them. As they dragged me to the shore and drowned me in the sea, I warned them. If they thought I was evil in life, that was nothing compared to the misery I'd rain down on them from the grave. I am the fury of the sea. And I will drown the world that drowned me."

She stretched out her arms gracefully like a ballet dancer and floated from the ground, rising four metres into the air. Water ran from her feet and splashed on the earth as she reached for the sky and seemed to pull downwards on something like an invisible rope.

A blinding flash stabbed Kirby's eyes. A fork of lightning crashed down, scorching the ground near Amelia's feet. The air was filled with the smell of burning grass as Amelia spun to face Kirby, to make sure he was alright. Her eyes grew wide as she realised her mistake.

Then everything stopped.

In reality, the storm was still raging as strong as ever. The wind was howling, the waves crashing, the rain battering the world. But now the three of them, Kirby, Amelia and the witch, were standing in a bubble of silence, separate from the storm, separate from the world.

Kirby, who'd fallen on his backside from the force of the lightning strike, slid up onto his knees and stared about. Raindrops hung in the air, motionless. He reached out a hand and touched them, picking them out of the sky and watching as they ran between his fingers. There was no wind, no lightning.

"You're afraid," the storm-witch said to Amelia. She sniffed at the air. "I can smell it. But you're not afraid of what I'm going to do to *you*, are you? No, you're ever so frightened of what I'll do to the boy."

In the calm, her features were clear and sharp and rather beautiful. She looked like an ice sculpture. She turned her head very slowly, and looked right at Kirby. "Hello," she said, in a voice that turned his heart to ice. He found he couldn't move, could barely breathe as she stared at him.

Then he heard a muffled scream from Amelia, and everything became distant and echoing and distorted. An icy sphere of water appeared around him, trapping him inside like a fish in a bowl. It enveloped him, stealing away his breath, which drifted up in clouds of bubbles around his head. Kirby thrashed and kicked, but he could not rupture the sphere. He was aware as he fought of movement outside, of flashes of lighting and faraway voices. Amelia would be trying to save him

– he knew that – but this last witch was different from the others.

Kirby's lungs screamed at him, begging for air.

*Hold on. Just hold on.*

His insides were on fire, his muscles straining to breathe.

*Help me, Amelia...*

His stomach heaved, his chest rising and falling in jerking movements as his body fought against him.

He closed his eyes. It was impossible to hold his breath any longer. He opened his mouth, let the water enter, and prepared to give in to his body's instinct...

The water collapsed around him. He dropped to the wet ground and sucked in great gulps of air. Every rasping breath was wonderful, tasting of salt and rain and life.

"Kirby!" Amelia's voice brought him to. She was standing five metres away, the storm still frozen all around. The witch was picking herself up off the soaking grass, her features re-forming. Then she was reaching for the sky again, pulling another lightning bolt towards the earth. White-hot lightning forked down towards Amelia. But instead of striking her and being over in a momentary flash, the blinding light remained.

Kirby, who had fallen back shielding his eyes, peeped through his fingers. The lightning had come only so far, stopping just inches above Amelia's head. It was spitting and crackling, shooting out sparks of electricity, turning the rain around it to steam. Kirby could feel the heat radiating from it. His hair stood on end.

Below the bolt of lightning stood Amelia. She did not move. She stared straight ahead, her eyes narrowed in concentration as she fought to keep the lightning bolt from hitting her.

Across the pocket of frozen storm, the witch screamed in effort, every part of her undulating, water dripping from her as if she was made from melting ice. The lightning licked at the air, inched downward, until it was so close to Amelia's head that her hair began to burn, and the sickening smell drifted towards Kirby.

*She's losing.*

*She can't lose.*

*I can't let her lose.*

He got to his feet and moved as close to Amelia as he could under the blinding light and intense heat. The lightning spat and crackled, almost speaking: *Burn... burn... burn...*

Amelia was sweating, her eyes still locked

straight ahead. Was she even aware he was beside her? Kirby looked across at the witch, and forced himself to speak.

"You're wrong!" he yelled. "I'm not Amelia's weakness. Since when is it weak to care about someone? Friends don't make you weak; they make you stronger. Friends help you do things you never thought you could. I know that better that anyone now..."

As Kirby spoke, the storm-witch grunted with effort and Amelia's eyes seemed to spark with new strength. Kirby edged closer to her, through the searing steam. He reached out and took Amelia's hand in his. "You can beat her," he said to her. "I'm here."

Something happened then – a change in the air and, most importantly, in Amelia. She smiled.

The scorching lightning jumped back slightly. The witch yelled and cursed.

Amelia continued to push back, and the fork of lighting began to bend away from her. It moved slowly at first, inches at a time. But as Amelia's strength grew it gathered momentum, and soon it was almost upon the storm-witch.

Steam rose from her watery body now; Kirby watched it twining off into the night. And as the lightning fork moved ever closer, her features started to bubble and churn until, with one final burst of strength from Amelia, it struck her down and she scattered into a million steaming droplets of rain.

Amelia collapsed to the ground. Kirby rushed to her side, wrapping an arm around her. Above, the storm clouds were parting. The wind died to a whisper. The rain stopped falling. The mist evaporated.

In just a few minutes, the night was clear and warm and still. Countless stars banded across the sky. The sea was calm. Summer had returned.

"She's gone," Kirby said. He sat with Amelia, who leaned her head on his shoulder and smiled a faraway smile. "We did it. We actually did it. Well, you did a bit more than me, I'll give you that, but they're gone. We're all safe."

"Ahem."

The cough was small and polite, and came from behind.

Brothers Swan and Swift stood in the moonlight. They began to applaud, wiping imaginary tears from their eyes.

"What a lovely moment," said Brother Swift, glaring through his stringy black hair.

"Yes," said Brother Swan. He smiled, showing a row of sharp brown teeth. "Shame we have to ruin it, isn't it?"

Brother Swift stepped forward, and smiled at Amelia. "Hello, Sister Pigeon," he said. "It's been a while."

# One Mistake

The standing stones were ancient. Kirby had once done a project on them in school. Nobody really knew for sure who had put them there or why, but they had been on the island since before people ever settled in Craghaven. They stood at the very centre of Ruby Island, bathed in the light of the moon.

After the roar of the storm everything seemed so silent, and the sweet smell of summer was in the air. Brother Swift led the way. He carried his sister Amelia over his shoulder; she was weak from fighting the last witch, and she did not put up a fight. Kirby followed behind them, with Brother Swan at the rear, holding a knife with a long, curved blade in his hands. Every now and then he would give Kirby a push or a kick up the backside.

Kirby was exhausted and soaked and frightened.

He kept hoping Amelia would make a move, but there was no sign of that.

When they reached the standing stones, the first thing Kirby noticed was the colour of the pillars. Even in the moonlight, they were a rich, deep red. "What's happened to them?"

"They were a tad drab," said Brother Swift, "so we thought we'd brighten them up a bit. Redecorate. Do you like it?"

Brother Swan ran a finger down one of the stones until his fingertip was coated red. Then he put it in his mouth and sucked the redness from it. "Blood is the loveliest shade of crimson, isn't it?"

Kirby shivered, and his breath caught in his throat. "That's blood? *Human* blood?"

"Sheep's blood," said Brother Swan, with an air of sadness in his voice. "My dear brother thought we'd attract too much attention if we used the human stuff." He turned his knife in the moonlight, causing the blade to glisten, and smiled at Kirby. "But there's still time."

Kirby stared at the point of the blade, and felt his body begin to shake.

Brother Swift heaved Amelia down from his shoulder and placed her on the grass. She managed to stand up, unsteady, swaying.

"I *trapped* you," she said, "in Egypt. How did you get out?"

"Patience," replied Brother Swift. "Lots and lots of patience."

"I'll end you. Both of you."

"Oh." Brother Swift gave a casual wave of his hand. "Normally I'd say you'd be quite capable of that. But not tonight, dear sister. Not after putting so much effort into that spectacular fight with our witch. She was rather special, wasn't she? The best of the bunch, I'd say."

"That's why you brought the witches back?" Amelia glowered at him. "To weaken me?"

"Right on the money as usual." Brother Swift nodded. "But we had to be careful. We didn't want to exhaust you completely. We needed to make sure you still had enough power for this – for what's to come."

Amelia glanced around, at the stones, at her brothers and at Kirby. Her eyes widened with a dawning realisation. "You can't!"

"Ah," said Brother Swift, "the penny drops at last! You're not as sharp as you used to be." He spun around, arms outstretched. "There's old magic in this place. Can you feel it, Sister Pigeon? Enough to open the door for Mother?"

"If you bring her back, she'll turn this world to dust."

"There was a time," said Brother Swift, "when you would have considered that a good thing. What happened to you, sister? What made you soft? Why do you care so much about these little people now?" He nodded to Kirby. "I've seen you make enough of them suffer over the years. Remember, Sister Pigeon. Remember how it felt when we were together, the four of us. All that power! All the wars and pain, just because we snapped our fingers and made it so!"

Amelia looked at Kirby, and her green eyes were filled with warmth and affection and tears. She smiled at him. "People like Kirby..." She nodded towards him, "are far stronger than we ever gave them credit for. They have a power you'll never understand, a power so strong nothing can break it – not fear, or suffering, or even death. They have love."

Brothers Swan and Swift looked at each other and shrugged.

"Well," said Brother Swift, brushing his long black hair from his eyes, "I'm moved. But look what your *love* has done for you. It's made you weak, made you vulnerable, made you think like one of them. You are a Shadowsmith, Sister Pigeon! Your sole purpose for being is to cast darkness, to weave it into the world, to balance out the light.

Mother will teach you that again. She'll make you remember."

Brother Swan's blade was now pressing against the skin of Kirby's throat, and Kirby was crying silently.

"Amelia," he said through the tears. Her eyes met his, burning green. "You saved me. I was lost and you made me feel like a person again. Whatever you did in the past, I forgive you. Because that wasn't the person I know. The person I know is strong and fair and good. You're *good,* Amelia. You bring hope and light. You make the world shine."

Brother Swan's skin took on a greenish hue and Brother Swift wiped away an imaginary tear from his eye. "That's quite enough of that," he said. "Any more and my brother may vomit. Now let's get to the point, shall we? You have a choice, Sister Pigeon. Help us bring Mother back from the void. She will forgive you for trapping her there, I'm certain of it. You are her child, after all, cut from her own shadow. If you do that, I promise you the boy will live. If, on the other hand, you walk away or try to fight us, you will lose, and the boy will die. And you know Brother Swan will take great pleasure in making sure his death is long and slow and lingering."

In one devastating moment, Kirby realised why the brothers had brought him to Ruby Island. He had been stupid to think he could ever help Amelia, when all the time he was being used as a bargaining chip.

"Amelia," he said, "leave me here. Don't give them what they wa—"

Brother Swan's hand clamped over Kirby's mouth.

Amelia stared at her brothers, cold hate in her eyes. "I want your word. Your *word* that he'll be spared."

"You have it," said Brother Swift with a bow.

Amelia gave a single nod.

*No! No no no—*

Kirby's scream was muffled.

These Shadowsmiths – Amelia and her brothers – were ancient, powerful creatures, and he couldn't begin to understand that power, not really. But he knew, deep in the pit of his soul, that if Mother came back, the Amelia he had come to know would be gone; she'd return to the shadows, and he'd lose her forever.

Desperate tears stinging his eyes, Kirby bit down hard on Brother Swan's hand, tasted his rotten flesh, and heard the yell pierce the night. Then he was free.

He made to run towards Amelia, but on his second stride he felt Brother Swan's hands in his hair. He was yanked backwards with a violent jerk, and pushed against one of the stranding stones with so much force the air was battered out of him.

Brother Swan's face was in Kirby's, his rancid breath making him gag. He leaned in close, whispering in Kirby's ear, "You can't move. Not a muscle. You're a statue."

The effect was immediate. Kirby tried to struggle but his body ignored him, every muscle, every fibre was frozen in place. He could not even blink away the tears. It was as if he had become one of the standing stones.

Then Brother Swan pressed the tip of his knife into Kirby's arm. Kirby tried to cry out as it pierced him, but he was a prisoner in his own body and the scream stayed in his head. A trickle of blood ran down his arm from the small cut Brother Swan had made.

Brother Swan took the knife, which was tipped with Kirby's blood, and wiped it on the standing stone, leaving a wet stain. "There we go. Just for luck, eh?"

Just then, Amelia looked at Kirby and winked.

# Mother

The stones were arranged in a circle. Amelia Pigeon and her brothers Swan and Swift stood an equal number of stones apart. For a long moment there was only the gentle sound of summer waves lapping against the cliffs. And then they began to speak, the three of them, in their ancient tongue. Their words drifted into the night and wrapped around everything. Kirby could feel them on his skin and in the air. He breathed them in, and they were in his blood and his mind, sharp and ragged. The air became heavy with words, so heavy it felt like the world might burst.

Unable to move, his eyes staring straight ahead, Kirby saw glimmers and flashes in the air at the centre of the stone circle, as if the moonlight was bouncing and warping around something invisible, something huge. A shadow came into being.

*No. Not a shadow,* thought Kirby. *Something else. A tear. A door to another place.*

And as Amelia's words mixed with those of her brothers, the tear in the world opened wider and pulled at the air. The moonlight grew dimmer, as if it was being dragged into the darkness.

A strange feeling crept over Kirby, a sensation of something leaving his body, and he realised that it was light, hope and happiness. They were all being ripped from him, feeding the void, to be replaced by fear and hopelessness.

The chanting grew in intensity. A great rumble came from the void. Kirby felt sweat running down his face, felt something reaching out towards him. He sensed it watching him, something ancient and powerful.

There came a sound so deep Kirby thought the ground was splitting, and a plume of black smoke shot out of the void high into the air, swirling, climbing. At first it was shapeless, but as it shifted and rolled, it began to take form.

There was a person in there – a giant – made of smoke, and with every passing second it was becoming more solid, becoming real. He could see the shape of a head, of ragged black robes.

From the smoke came a voice, and it was

everywhere – in Kirby's ears, in his head, hissing, grating, ripping at his senses. MY CHILDREN.

"Yes, Mother!" said Brother Swan, his arms outstretched, his face alight with joy.

"O Despicable One!" screamed Brother Swift. "O Supreme Bringer of Darkness! Mummy!"

YOU'VE LET THE PLACE GO.

The brothers exchanged worried looks. "We've tried, Mother. Oh, we've tried!"

NOT HARD ENOUGH.

The brothers wailed and cowered to the ground as Mother glared down at them.

The smoke swirled so that the thing inside was facing Amelia. AND YOU! MY OWN DAUGHTER! YOU TRICKED ME. SENT ME TO THE NOTHINGNESS. YOU'LL SUFFER. YOU'LL SCREAM AND BEG. THEN YOU'LL COME BACK TO MY SIDE.

Amelia dropped to her knees, clutching at her head, crying in pain.

Kirby strained against the spell, horror and fear slashing at his insides as he stared up at the monster in the smoke.

And then there was Amelia's voice, in his head. "Kirby," she said. "Kirby, be strong, be brave. They made a mistake. A big mistake. They used your blood and they let you live. The magic of the spell is part of you now. Feel it. Use it. Stop her." The words, silent to the rest of the world, drifted around Kirby's mind, and there they anchored and grew. He could feel their warmth flowing through him, their power.

He moved his eyes first, shifting his gaze sideward to Amelia. She was still on her knees, crying in pain, but she was staring intently at him.

Kirby gained more control over his body. He pushed and pushed, until he broke free from the standing stone, the force of the spell flowing in his veins.

He glanced over at her brothers, who were clinging to each other and weeping.

Then he dared to look up at the smoke figure, which turned its head towards him.

WHAT HAVE WE HERE?

He felt the creature's strength grow as its dark robes gradually became more substantial, swishing in the soft breeze. Soon she'd close the tear, and she'd be unstoppable.

Kirby knew what he had to do. It was written in his every thought, as if it was meant to be this way. He looked once more at Amelia, and he thought of Mum and Dad and Craghaven.

Then he ran forward, and leapt into the void.

# The Void

Darkness.

Kirby knew he was still Kirby. He could remember. He recalled Mum and Dad, and Amelia, and the smell of the sea. He remembered his bedroom and how the summer sun felt on his skin. He remembered exactly what had been going through his head in the moments before he leapt into the tear.

In this place, wherever he was, he did not have a body.

It was the strangest sensation, like being everywhere at once, spread out into infinity. And he knew something was sharing the space with him, something that watched him with a curious eye.

He thought he'd try to speak, because that's what a person would do, isn't it? Shout into the dark and hope something can hear you.

Surprisingly, he found he had a voice. "I know you're in here."

Silence.

"I'm not really sure what you are," he went on. "I won't pretend to understand how strong you are, or how many bad things you've done. But I understand one thing very clearly. I'm here to stop you causing any more harm."

WHAT ARE YOU?

If a dying star could speak, this is how its voice would sound. It was huge, and burning, and empty of everything but fury.

"I'm one of the little people," said Kirby. "I think that's what you call us."

A pause.

IMPOSSIBLE.

He could feel Mother in every inch of the darkness, probing him with her thoughts, trying to break into his mind. In the world he knew, she would have crushed him like he was nothing. But not here, not now.

"I should be frightened of you," he said. "And I am. I'm really, really frightened. But you know what? Out there, where I'm from, there are people I need to protect."

The darkness bristled. Kirby pushed on.

"Your sons made a mistake. They made me part of the spell that's supposed to bring you back.

So here I am. Standing in your way. I won't let you past, even if I have to guard the way forever."

She pushed harder, and he felt the pressure. She was creeping in on him, twining around his mind in the dark. He pushed back.

I HAVE SEEN WORLDS BORN AND DIE. I HAVE OUTLIVED STARS AND GODS AND CIVILISATIONS. YOU WILL BREAK.

She pushed again, and Kirby felt her grip tighten. Her creeping roots were forcing their way into his thoughts.

YES, she said. BREAK.

Flashes in his mind. Dad out on the lifeboat, enormous waves swallowing the boat up, dragging it down into the dark sea.

"No," he said, feeling the fear infecting him. "That's not happening, not real."

Another image. Mum in her hospital bed, machines beeping, alarms screaming. Nurses and doctors crowding around, trying to save her. And then stepping back, shaking their heads...

"No!" Kirby yelled.

And now a coffin being lowered into the ground, Kirby standing alone at Mum's grave in the cold and the rain...

She pushed again, almost breaking past him.

Kirby was so close to defeat.

Then, in the vision of the graveside, he felt a warm hand take his, and he saw a yellow raincoat and a freckled face and green eyes. In the darkness he saw light. Warmth flowed through him, and he forced the visions to change...

He saw Dad coming ashore, safe, alive. He felt Mum wrapping her arms around him.

Mother's grip loosened. She fell back.

"You'll never win," he said, and this time his voice was as fierce and bright as the birth of a star. He forced her out of his thoughts, forced her deeper and deeper into the void. "There are people who love me. People who need me. I won't let you win!"

An explosion of light illuminated the dark. He felt her shrinking and cowering.

YOU CAN'T KEEP ME OUT FOREVER. I'LL FIND A WAY...

Kirby screamed out with one final effort, and she fell away into infinity.

After that there was only silence, and light.

Something pulled at him. He was falling, falling, falling.

He landed on wet grass.

Above him, the tear in everything was no longer black. It was shining bright as the sun. And the column of smoke was formless again, being sucked into the light.

It took him a few moments to feel his body again. He scrambled away clumsily to the outer edge of the stone circle.

Amelia was sitting on the grass, shaking away the cobwebs. Around her, Brothers Swan and Swift were trying desperately to run away, but the tear was pulling them back, drawing them in.

"No! Oh please no!"

Their feet slipped and slid on the grass, their heels dug in. They wrapped their arms around the standing stones, but the spell was too strong and their fingernails left marks in the stone as they grasped and scratched. The void would not be denied a meal. It wrenched them to the ground and they grabbed at the long grass, ripping up clumps of earth.

Brother Swift was sucked in first.

"I'm sorry!" he yelled. "I'll be good!" It pulled him in by the legs, screaming and kicking, swallowing him up.

Brother Swan was next, the light from the void reflecting off his bald head as he disappeared, limb by limb, until only his face was left, distorted and terrified.

"We'll come back," he said. "We'll find a way..." And a final burst of suction gobbled him too.

The tear closed up, folding in on itself until, with a final shimmer, it was gone.

*They* were gone.

The sounds of Kirby's world returned: the sea on the rocks and the breeze in the long grass. Even the moonlight seemed to sing.

Amelia sat beside him on the ground, and kissed him on the cheek.

"I think," she said, "it's time to go home."

# Going Home

There were two moons: one in the sky, the other reflected in the shimmering calmness of the North Sea. Dad's little lobster boat cut through the water, Amelia at the wheel in her yellow raincoat. There were dark rings around her eyes and a gash on her head, but as the boat moved ever further from Ruby Island towards the warm twinkling lights of Craghaven, she smiled.

Kirby watched her every move. He was not scared of her. He could never imagine she would do anything to hurt him. But after the events on the island, he could not help but think of her differently. She was not a girl, not at all, no matter how she smiled at him or how her hair shone.

"How old are you really?" he asked.

She stared right ahead at the water. The boat's engine hummed. "Honestly, I don't know. I lost count."

"But you're old? Like Swan and Swift said?"

"Yes."

A pause.

"If she had come back… your mother… how bad would that have been?"

This time Amelia looked at him, looked right into his eyes, and her green eyes were fierce. "Worse than you can imagine. She'd have dragged the world back to the shadows. It's what Shadowsmiths are for – to balance out the good with bad, the light with dark. To provide chaos." She looked away again, unable to hold his gaze.

Kirby thought for a minute, then he said, "Dad always says nobody should be ashamed of where they come from. He was in jail, you know, my dad. A long time ago, way before I was born. For stealing a car."

"I did a lot worse than steal a car, Kirby."

"I know that. I do. But every single day since he got in trouble, my dad has been working to make up for it, and to be the best person he can be. And I think that's what you're doing too, when you go around helping people like me. You're putting things right, and you won't ever stop. And that makes you brave."

There were tears in Amelia's eyes. "Does it?"

"I think it does," he said.

"And what about you?" she said. "You stood up to her. There's not another person alive who's done that. What did you tell her?"

Kirby shrugged. "I told her I would guard the way forever if I had to. And I showed her the people I love. I showed her what I'm fighting for."

Amelia smiled again. "You, boy, are much smarter than you look. And isn't that a blessing?"

They laughed, long and loud, and the lobster boat sailed on towards home.

Mrs Coppershot's living room light was still on, casting a warm glow through thin curtains.

"Here we are," said Kirby.

"Yes," said Amelia. "Here we are." She looked exhausted, but her eyes were sparkling. In the east, the first shoots of dawn were creeping skyward. "A new day."

"It feels like a new day," said Kirby. "Everything's bright and shiny again."

"Thanks to you."

Kirby nodded. "You have to leave, don't you?"

"I do."

"Right now?"

"No, not right now. First I have to rest, and you should too. But after that, there are other things I need to do. Other places to go. Other people who need help."

"Would it be really selfish to ask you to stay for one more adventure?"

"Not selfish, but not possible either." Amelia nodded towards Mrs Coppershot's red front door. "Go in. Get some sleep. I won't leave without saying goodbye, I promise."

Kirby turned and looked at the house, and he knew before he turned back that Amelia would be gone. He smiled and unlocked the door, entering the warmth of Mrs Coppershot's house.

The old lady was still asleep in her armchair, snoring so loudly the walls were almost shaking. Kirby picked up the teacups Brothers Swan and Swift had used earlier, took them into the kitchen and washed them up. Then he ate a packet of prawn cocktail crisps, had a large glass of milk, and went back to the living room and lay on the couch. As soon as he closed his eyes, he was asleep.

"Kirby?"

"Mmm?"

"Kirby."

Someone was shaking him.

"I'm sleeping."

"Aye, I can see that. Come on. Time to go home, sunshine."

"I'm com-fy. Five more min-utes."

"Come on, pal. Up."

Kirby's eyes opened and took a moment to make sense of what he was seeing.

"Dad?"

"Alright, pal?"

"Dad!"

Kirby leapt up and grabbed his dad in the tightest hug he could manage.

"Whoa! I've only been away for a few hours!"

"Feels a lot longer," said Kirby.

"Told you I'd come back, didn't I? Takes more than a wee storm to keep your old dad down."

"Did you find them?" Kirby asked. "The ship that called for help?"

"We did, aye. Crew's all safe and sound. Knocked a bit loopy by the storm mind you." He shook his head. "Man, you should have seen the weather out there! I've never known anything like it. And there was some crazy lightning out by Ruby Island."

Kirby smiled. "Really? I wish I'd seen that."

They said goodbye to Mrs Coppershot, who was back to her normal self, and did not remember anything about Brothers Swan or Swift. She gave them a plate full of homemade chocolate-chip cookies.

Things really did feel different: the summer air was warm and sweet, and the sound of the sea was soothing. It was almost morning, and the sky was every colour of blue you could imagine. The last of the stars were scattered to the west.

"I'm starving," said Kirby, as Dad opened the door.

"Me too." Dad held up Mrs Coppershot's plate. "Be rude not to sample a couple of these, wouldn't it? I mean good old Mrs Coppershot went to the trouble of baking them..."

They closed the door.

Both Kirby and Dad were completely unaware that something was watching from the rooftops.

# Goodbye

Mum would wake up now. Kirby was sure of it. The witches were gone, and Swan and Swift were beaten. There was no dark magic left hanging over her, or Craghaven.

When they got to the hospital the next day, Kirby galloped to Mum's room and threw open the door, expecting her to be sitting up, waiting with open arms.

He was greeted by the familiar beep of the machines. Mum was lying perfectly still, as she had been for so long. The doctors gave the usual update. No change.

Kirby struggled through the visit. When he got home he ran to his room, buried his face in his pillow, and cried and cried and cried until he fell asleep.

When he woke up he felt a bit better. He went over everything in his mind – every witch, every battle. He'd done all of it to help Mum. So why hadn't it?

If only he could ask Amelia.

No sign of her, either.

A week went by.

There were reports on the television and in the newspapers about what the press had decided to call the 'Weather Bomb'. Experts and conspiracy theorists waffled on about the cause, their theories ranging from global warming to aliens.

Dad taught Kirby how to play chess, and soon he was winning his share of the games, but he could never quite tell if he was really winning or if Dad was letting him win. By the end of the week the crushing disappointment of Mum not waking up had numbed a little. Kirby read to her every day, and Dad listened and enjoyed it. He didn't even take a newspaper into the room any more.

Summer, it seemed, was here to stay this time. The world baked in its heat, and everything smelled of barbecues, dry grass and ice cream. The government announced that there would be a hosepipe ban, which meant people could not use hoses to wash their cars or sprinklers to keep their grass green – to save water. Dad said this hadn't happened for years.

On one of those glorious days, Kirby walked down the street, past the harbour to the crescent-shaped beach at Ruby Cove. He took off his trainers and stepped into the water. Usually the North Sea was grey as steel and cold enough to turn a person blue in a few minutes. But today it was pleasant and warm as it lapped against Kirby's shins.

He stared out to Ruby Island. Had it all really happened? It seemed so long ago, so far away.

The back of his neck prickled.

Someone was watching.

He turned around, looking back to the beach, and there she was, in her dazzling yellow raincoat.

"I reckon it might be safe to lose the coat, you know." He pointed to the forever-blue sky.

"I like this raincoat," she said. "It's a *nice* raincoat."

Kirby sat on the sand and let his feet dry in the warm breeze. Amelia sat beside him.

"How are you, Kirby?"

A pause.

"Mum didn't wake up."

Amelia shook her head sadly. "Oh, Kirby. I told you not to pin all your hopes on that. I'm so sorry."

"I was just so sure it would work," said Kirby. "And now it hasn't... I don't know what else to do."

Amelia sighed and put a hand on his shoulder. "Sometimes the hardest thing is admitting that there's nothing you can do."

Kirby stared out towards the calm blue sea.

After a while he said, "I asked Dad if I could have my own fishing rod."

"Well... that's good."

"Yeah. I just thought: you know what, if I can rid the world of an all-consuming evil, then why should I be frightened of a little bit of water?"

Amelia gave him a bright smile. Her freckles connected. "You've seen a few strange things lately."

"I've seen a *lot* of strange things," Kirby corrected her.

"I guess you might wish you could forget a few of them?"

Kirby raised an eyebrow. "Oh no. No way! You're not taking any of my memories!"

She held up her hands innocently. "Look, I'm just saying. Seeing the things you've seen... knowing the secrets you know about the world... it's a heavy load for a person to carry around."

"But I *want* to carry it. I *want* to remember."

She gave him a doubtful look. "I don't know."

"Well I do," said Kirby. "I know I'm not scared of everything any more. I know I've got my dad back. I know whatever happens to Mum I'm more prepared than before. I don't want to forget the things that helped me. I want to remember them, and see them whenever I need to."

Amelia pursed up her mouth. She folded her arms.

"And..." Kirby looked at his feet, "I don't want to forget about you. You don't forget friends, Amelia. Every time I see a horrible yellow raincoat, no matter where I am, I want it to remind me of you."

Amelia put two fingers in her mouth and pretended she was being sick. "Fine," she said. "You win."

Kirby smiled. They sat on the beach for a while, the tide rising and the sound of the gulls in the air.

At last, she said, "I have to go."

"I know."

They stood and faced each other, and Amelia reached into her trusty yellow raincoat and pulled out a hazel twig. She held it out. "Just in case."

Kirby took it.

She brushed her hair from her green eyes, and she leaned in and kissed him on the cheek. Kirby felt his face go red.

"You're going to do great things, Kirby Simpson. I'll keep an eye out for you."

"Kirby!" Dad was standing on the harbour wall, waving. "Visiting time, pal! Come on."

Kirby waved back. When he turned again, the only sign Amelia had ever been there was a message written with a stick in the sand.

# FIVE

# Life Goes On

# A Familiar Face

Kirby and Dad sat at a table by the window in Frankie's Café. It was Saturday morning in Craghaven, and the water was calm and blue.

"You OK?" Dad asked as he cut into a slice of black pudding and shovelled it into his mouth.

Kirby looked over his stack of pancakes. "Yeah," he said. "Why?"

Dad tilted his head. "You haven't mentioned your friend lately – the girl. What's her name? Emily?"

"Amelia."

"Aye, Amelia." He scooped up a pile of scrambled egg and sausage. "Where is she?"

Kirby pushed a bit of pancake around his plate. "She had to go."

Dad nodded, as if he'd seen this sort of thing a hundred times. "Aye, that's the thing with living at the seaside," he said. "People come and go quicker than the tide. You liked her, eh?"

"Yeah..." Kirby paused then added, "but not like that. She wasn't my girlfriend or anything."

"Whatever you say, pal," said Dad with a smile. Then the smile faded. "You will tell me, from now on, won't you? When there's something wrong? We can do that now, you and me?"

Kirby nodded. "I will. I promise."

After breakfast Dad had some errands to run around town.

"Sure you don't want to come?"

"Shopping? No thanks. I think I'll go for a walk."

"Suit yourself. Just make sure you're back in plenty of time for visiting."

Kirby went to Ruby Cove first. He'd been there most days since Amelia left. He stood on the spot they'd last spoken and chucked some stones into the water, seeing how far he could throw.

*Typical,* he thought, *first real friend I ever make and she's not even human.*

He reached down and rolled up the leg of his jeans. The hazel wand Amelia had given him was safely tucked down his sock. He brought it out and ran his fingers along the rough bark.

He wondered, as he'd done so many times, where Amelia was now. What kind of trouble would she find? What sort of adventures was she having? And was she having them with someone else, someone who wasn't him?

He walked up the steep series of winding roads through Craghaven and then out of the village, past the field where the carnival had been a few weeks ago. He wasn't really thinking about where he was going. He just kept walking, along a narrow dirt road between two of Farmer Weir's fields then through a field of high corn, a golden sea waving in the breeze around him. At last, he came to the point where the farm met the woods. He saw the old farmhouse, boarded up and abandoned, and he realised he'd known where he was going all along.

A sudden, searing pain engulfed his hand. He grabbed it, and examined it. On the fleshy part of his palm, where the spider had once been, there was a bright pink scar. Kirby looked around, his heartbeat picking up. A voice in his head was telling him to turn around, to run. He didn't listen.

The farmhouse door was stiff, as it had been last time, and right before it cracked open a rush of hope bubbled up inside him. Maybe he'd open the door to find Amelia waiting in her impossible kitchen, cooking eggs and yelling at him for tracking her down again.

But all that waited inside was the empty silence of a lonely old house.

Kirby entered, looked around.

A floorboard creaked.

"You can still feel her here, can't you?"

The voice made him jump. He stared hard into the shadows.

"I can feel her too," said a voice that was eerily familiar...

"Who's there?" Kirby asked.

A movement in the dark. Bright beams of sunlight pierced through gaps in the boarded-up windows. The person walking towards Kirby stepped into a sunbeam so that Kirby could see his face.

Kirby took a sharp breath. He stepped back, once, twice, until he hit the wall.

"This isn't real." Beads of cold sweat were forming on his face. His scalp was crawling, and the blood in his veins was tingling with fear. The person who'd come from the shadows, the person standing only a few metres away from him, couldn't be there, not really.

When Kirby looked across the kitchen he saw his own features staring back – his eyes and nose and mouth, his hair and clothes, his voice, his face.

There were two Kirby Simpsons in the farmhouse.

# One More Fight

Two Kirbys. Impossible.

And yet, after everything he'd seen, not impossible at all. And that made it all the more frightening. This wasn't some nightmare he could just wake up from.

"What are you?" he said, still pressed against the kitchen wall.

"You know what I am," said the second Kirby.

"I don't. I really, really don't."

The second Kirby smiled, and Kirby noticed for the first time that they were not quite identical; this Kirby, the fake, had a long scar running down the side of his face.

The second Kirby saw him looking, and ran his finger down the scar. "This?" he said. "You gave me this. Have you forgotten?"

"I didn't do that. I wouldn't."

The fake Kirby smiled. There were other differences too. Kirby could see them now, as his eyes adjusted to the dim light. The second Kirby's eyes were sunken into his head and there were dark rings around them. He was thinner, more angular, slightly stooped.

"It happened in the fairground." The second Kirby pointed to his face. "You did this – in the haunted house, with a piece of witch-stick. It burned."

Kirby stared at his other self, then at the scar on his hand. "You're the *spider*?"

"If that's what you want to call me."

"So how come you look like *me*?"

The second Kirby smiled. "When you attacked our nest, I hid in your flesh. You carried me out of danger."

Kirby stared at the place on his palm where the spider had burst through his skin.

"I took a part of you when I left that night," said the fake Kirby. "It made me stronger, and it let me come out in the sunlight. Let me look like this."

"Why?" said Kirby.

The second Kirby stared hard at him. "You took away my family. All my brothers and sisters died in the cave that night."

Kirby edged towards the door. "They didn't belong here," he said. "They were going to hurt people."

"They're gone because of *you*." The second Kirby smiled crookedly. "But the Shadowsmith isn't here to protect you this time, is she?" He took another step. "I've been to visit your mum, you know."

Kirby stopped moving towards the door. "You what?"

"Oh yes, we've had a few chats, her and I. Well, when I say chats... she's not really much of a talker at the moment, is she?"

"You stay away!" Kirby shook his fists. "Leave her!"

"You cleaned this town up. Got rid of all the darkness. Except me."

"What do you want?"

"I want to take away your mother, like you took away mine."

"Your mother?"

"In the nest in the cave. You sent her to a watery grave."

In his head, Kirby saw the spider's nest again, saw the huge thing squirming inside.

"I'm going to wrap you up in a web," said the fake, "and leave you with just enough strength to watch your mum lose her battle."

They stood perfectly still, staring at each other, waiting to see who would be the first to make a move.

Kirby reached down for the hazel wand in his sock, quick as he could. He had it in his fingers, but before he could use it, the second Kirby leapt across the room and knocked him to the ground. He landed with a heavy thud on the wooden floor, and the hazel fell out of his grasp.

"Where's your friend now, eh? Where's the Shadowsmith?"

Then the second Kirby's hands were pulling him up so they were eye to eye. Kirby pushed him away as hard as he could, and made a run for the wand, but the fake Kirby tripped him. He grabbed Kirby's leg and dragged him out of the kitchen, through the hallway to another room, where the skeleton of a burned-out armchair sat in one corner and a shattered mirror stood leaning against the wall.

Kirby kicked and scratched and fought. He broke free and scrambled across the room, crouching under the boarded-up window. The fake Kirby edged closer, his fingers twitching. In the fragments of the shattered mirror, Kirby saw the fake's reflection, and it was not the reflection of a boy. It was a midnight-black spider, the size of a large rat.

"You frightened, Kirby?" said the spider-boy. "I can smell it. I can hear your heart."

Kirby stood up, and they circled each other until

Kirby was sure the broken mirror was directly behind him. Then he said, "Come on then."

The second Kirby yelled and charged at him, but Kirby was waiting. He dodged out of the way, sending the fake through what was left of the broken mirror. He yelled out in shock and pain as the ragged glass cut him.

Kirby was out of the room in a flash, into the kitchen, grabbing the hazel wand, and then out the door of the old farmhouse, back into the warm golden sunshine.

An idea struck him then. He did not have Amelia by his side. He couldn't use magic to beat this thing. So he'd have to use cunning instead. But he'd have to be quick if it was to work. He hid the real hazel wand in his sock then he ran to the nearest tree and snapped off a branch. Clutching the new stick in his hand, he hurried through the field of high, swaying corn, the brightness of the world stinging his eyes.

"You can't get away!" came the second Kirby's voice from somewhere back in the field. "Not ever!"

Out of the field Kirby ran, across the main road and into a second field where the corn was even taller. The stalks whipped his face as he ran, each breath filling his lungs with warm summer air that tasted of the farm and the sea.

He could hear the fake Kirby brushing through the corn behind him.

And then there was no more corn. He was out in the open and just ahead was the very edge of the land. The cliffs. He turned, his pulse pounding in his ears, and waited.

The fake Kirby stepped from the cornfield like a ghost. "Nowhere to run." He took a step forward.

Kirby held out the branch he'd just taken from the tree. The fake Kirby stopped.

"I'll tell you what," said Kirby, "I'll fight you, fair and square. No spidery stuff from you. No webs. No venom. No fangs. And no wand for me."

"I don't need tricks to beat you." The second Kirby smiled. "I was forged in endless darkness. I am a living shadow, a nightmare."

Kirby faked a yawn. "Yeah, so you keep telling me." He drew his arm back and threw the twig away, over the edge of the cliff to the sea far, far below. Then he turned back to the spider-boy. "Now prove it."

The second Kirby was in no great rush. He sauntered up, so that they stood face to face. Then he looked at his hand as if it was something foreign to him, which of course it was, and he curled his fingers into a fist. He swung.

Kirby had been counting on that. The force of

the blow hit him square on the side of the head. He fell to the ground, his ear ringing. Then he took his chance.

He reached down into his sock, and pulled out the real hazel wand. Quick as he could, he drew a circle on the ground, around himself and the spider.

As soon as the circle was complete, the second Kirby began to scream. He tried to move out of it, but Kirby jumped to his feet and grabbed him, holding him as tight and as close as he could. The fake Kirby squealed and kicked and thrashed. His skin began to bubble. His hair burned. Kirby clung on with everything he had, every muscle straining to keep the melting creature inside the circle.

The fake Kirby looked him in the eye, fury and pain etched on his face, and he said, "You tricked me."

"You threatened my family."

The fake Kirby stopped fighting. He shrunk in Kirby's arms, and his body began to twist and transform until a spider the size of a large rat was writhing and spitting on the ground, its legs twitching madly.

When the spider finally stopped moving, it turned slowly to ash, and Kirby watched the warm breeze lifting it, scattering the ash far and wide, over the edge of the cliff to the sky and the sea.

Kirby dropped to his knees, struggling to catch his breath. He lay flat out on the ground, the sound of the waves in his head. He held the hazel stick up and stared at it. Amelia's words echoed in his mind.

"Just in case."

The walk home took him longer than usual because his leg was stiff from the fight. Along the way, his mind raced. He realised he was being selfish, wishing Amelia would come back, because he was strong enough to do without her now. There were other people who needed her. And he wondered, now that the last connection to Swan and Swift and the storm was gone... would it change anything?

He reached the front door of his house, unlocked it, and was about to step inside when he heard Mrs Coppershot's voice.

"Kirby! Kirby, thank goodness!"

She was moving up the street as quickly as she could, which wasn't very quick at all. When she reached him she grabbed him by the shoulders.

"Where've you been? Your dad was in a frenzy!"

"Frenzy? Why?"

"He had to go to the hospital. They phoned him in.

I've to take you there straight away!"

Sickness rose in Kirby's throat. "Why? Mrs Coppershot, what's happened?"

"I don't know. All he told me was he had to go right away and we were to follow as soon as I found you."

Kirby shook his head. "No." Tears began to come. "*No.*"

Mrs Coppershot hugged him. "We don't know anything yet. Until we do there'll be none of that, thank you."

"Why else would Dad rush off without me?"

"Come on," said Mrs Coppershot. "In the car."

# Family

Mrs Coppershot's car was a Mini. Not one of the fancy new ones, but an original Mini. It was mustard yellow, with shiny little hubcaps and cream-leather seats. Any other time Kirby had been in the car with her, Mrs Coppershot had driven slowly and with great care. Today, she drove like she'd been possessed by a demon.

The little car flew along the country roads, round twists and turns and over hills with the tyres barely staying on the tarmac. They screeched into a parking space at the hospital and burst through the doors, Mrs Coppershot hobbling to keep up.

The lift seemed to take an age to climb to the right floor. When the doors began to open, Kirby squeezed through, sprinting along the corridor to the room Mum was in. He stopped dead, his trainers squeaking on the polished floor, the clean, cold smell of bleach and chemicals everywhere.

The door to Mum's room was shut. The curtains were drawn.

Mrs Coppershot put a hand on his shoulder. "I'll wait here, love. You go."

Kirby nodded absently. He walked forward, feeling like this was happening to someone else. He stopped at the door, put his hand on the handle, and took a deep breath.

He opened the door.

The room was bright with sunshine.

Dad was sitting by the side of Mum's bed, holding her hand.

She was still. She looked peaceful.

Dad looked up, met Kirby's gaze. He smiled, and wiped the tears from his eyes. "I was looking for you."

"Yeah," said Kirby. "I went for a wander. Sorry."

He walked around to the side of the bed, and he took Mum's hand.

Her hand was warm.

And it squeezed his hand back.

Kirby's head shot up. He looked at his dad, wide-eyed, his chest filling with hope.

"It happened around lunchtime." Dad shook

his head and chuckled. He was crying, but these were good tears.

Kirby looked down at Mum. Her eyes opened a little. Not much, but enough that he could see the blue. And the corners of her mouth turned up in a half-smile. She squeezed his hand again.

"Kirby," she said softly.

A laugh escaped from Kirby's chest. He wiped his eyes again and leaned over and kissed her on the forehead, his heart fit to burst.

"Hi, Mum," he said. "We've missed you."

# The Next Stop

In a house in the backstreets of London, a doorbell rang.

Nobody answered at first.

The doorbell rang again. And again.

A door creaked open on the upstairs landing.

A moment later, a girl crept down the stairs. As she moved towards the front door, she glanced into the living room. There were empty beer bottles on the floor, and she could hear snoring from the couch and the blare of daytime TV.

When she reached the door, she looked through the peephole.

There was a girl outside. She was wearing a bright yellow raincoat, which was strange considering they were in the middle of the hottest July in ten years.

The girl opened the door.

The girl in the yellow raincoat smiled at her.

"Who are you?" asked the girl in the house.

"Hello, Stacey. My name's Amelia Pigeon." She paused, and smiled again. "Are you brave?"

READ ON
TO ENTER...

THE
NOWHERE
EMPORIUM

ROSS MACKENZIE

The shop from nowhere arrived with the dawn on a crisp November morning.

Word travelled quickly around the village, and by midday the place was abuzz with rumour and hearsay.

*"There were four shops in the row yesterday. Today there are five!"*

*"Did you hear? It sits between the butcher's and the ironmonger's…"*

*"The brickwork is black as midnight, and it sparkles strangely in the light!"*

By evening time, a curious crowd had begun to gather around the mysterious building. They jostled for position and traded strange and wonderful theories about where the shop had come from and what it might sell, all the while hoping to catch a glimpse of movement through the darkened windows.

The shop was indeed built from bricks the colour of midnight, bricks that shimmered and sparkled under the glow of the gas streetlamps. Blocking the doorway was a golden gate so fine and intricate that some wondrous spider might have spun it. Over the windows, curling letters spelled out a name:

There was a glimmer of movement in the entranceway, and a ripple of excitement passed through the crowd. And then silence fell – a silence so deep and heavy that it seemed to hang in the atmosphere like mist.

The shop's door swung open. The fine golden gate turned to dust, scattering in the wind.

The air was suddenly alive with a hundred scents: the perfume of toasted coconut and baking bread; of salty sea air and freshly fallen rain; of bonfires and melting ice.

A dove emerged from the darkness of the shop and soared through the air, wings flashing white in the blackness. The enchanted crowd watched as it climbed until it was lost to the night. And then, as one, they gasped. The black sky exploded with light and colour, and a message in dazzling firework sparks and shimmers spelled out:

**THE NOWHERE EMPORIUM**
**IS OPEN FOR BUSINESS.**
**BRING YOUR IMAGINATION...**

The writing hung in the air just long enough for everyone to read it, and then the words began falling to the ground, a rain of golden light. The crowd laughed in delight, reaching out to catch the sparks as they fell.

Everybody who'd gathered outside the Emporium was entranced. No one had ever seen a spectacle such as this. One by one they walked forward, touched the sparkling black brickwork, examined the tips of their fingers. And then they stepped through the door to find out what was waiting.

Two days later, when the shop had vanished, a stranger arrived in the village. He was polite, and he paid for his room with stiff new banknotes. But something about him – his startling height perhaps, or the hungry look in his cold blue eyes – troubled the villagers.

He asked questions about a shop built from midnight bricks.

But the tall man couldn't find a single person in the village who could recall the Emporium.

Within a day he too was gone, and all trace of these strange events faded from the history of the place.

Those who'd walked through the Emporium's doors had no memory of anything they might have seen inside. More importantly, none of them recalled the price of admission – the little piece of themselves they'd given for a glimpse at the Emporium's hidden secrets and wonders.

*Bring your imagination,* the sign in the sky had requested.